Secretary's Punishment

J.W. MCKENNA

SECRETARY'S PUNISHMENT

2008

Secretary's Punishment

OTHER BOOKS BY J.W. MCKENNA

The Hunted*
Darkest Hour*
Slave Planet*
Lord of Avalon
Naughty Girl*
The Cameo
Wanted: Kept Woman*
Bird in a Cage
My Pet*
Delicious Blackmail
Private Daydreams
Corruption of an Innocent Girl
Office Slave*
Office Slave II: El Exposed*
Controlled!
Out of Control
Out of Control II
Sold into Slavery
The Politician's Wife*
Abduction of Isobelle
My Husband's Daddy*
My Wife's Master*
Remedial Sybian Training*
Torn Between Two Masters*
Two Girls in Trouble

The Sex Slave Protocols*

*Available in print as well as ebook form

For details, visit: <u>www.jwmckenna.com</u>

BOOK 1

Emily

CHAPTER ONE

Congratulations. You got the job," said the prim, fifty-something human resources manager, looking over the top of her glasses at the pretty young woman seated in front of her. "Welcome to Bonham Industries."

Emily Robinson was so thrilled she could barely contain her excitement. It had been three months since she'd been laid off from her previous job and her savings had just about run out. She had begun to wonder if moving to St. Louis had been a mistake. Somehow, by luck or by the strength of her two interviews, she had made it!

"Thank you so much, Mrs. Dowd—I'll do a real good job for you, I promise," she gushed at the woman.

"Yes, well…" Mrs. Dowd seemed uncomfortable. She took off her glasses and folded them carefully in her hands. "You should know that you'll be the administrative assistant to Mr. Caudry, one of our senior salesmen. He, uh, can be, er, difficult."

In her mind, Emily pictured a crotchety old man who thought of all young people as "whippersnappers." Still, she would not be dissuaded from her good mood. "Oh, I'm sure we'll get along. I get along with everyone."

Mrs. Dowd nodded and bit her lip. "Um, good. Well, we have some paperwork for you to fill out, then I'll begin your orientation."

Emily filled out the information for health insurance and a 401(k) plan and was handed an employee's manual. Everything was so exciting and new! She almost hummed to herself as she completed the forms.

"That should do it," Mrs. Dowd said. "Now, let me show you how the phone and computer work." Over the next forty-five minutes, Emily took notes as she tried to keep up with the dizzying rash of instructions the woman tossed out. Everything was simultaneously straight-forward and complex. Filling out the calendar for her new boss's movements should have been easy, except for the codes she had to memorize to use the program. And the phone! It was so high-tech she could probably call up satellites with it but all she wanted to understand was how to get an outside line.

With her head still spinning, she suddenly realized Mrs. Dowd had stood. Emily rose to her feet at once, feeling butterflies in her stomach. "Any questions?"

Emily had too many to ask and realized at the same time that "none" was the correct answer. She shook her head.

"Good. Follow me."

Mrs. Dowd led the way through the warren of cubicles, pausing to point out a conference room, the bathrooms and the employee lounge. Emily was aware of many eyes on her and tried to nod and smile in response. Mrs. Dowd came to a section where three offices lined the far wall. They were all faced with rich wood paneling. Thick carpeting padded the floor, setting the area off from the common cubicle farm. Mrs. Dowd stopped at the first desk just outside an oak door. "This will be your spot."

Emily opened her eyes wide in disbelief—she had just been hired and already she was assigned as administrative assistant in such a cushy spot? She looked past Mrs. Dowd to the cubicles and then back to the woman, confused.

"Yes, I know what you're thinking—why are you here instead of one of those other girls? Someone who has been here longer? Am I right?"

Emily could only nod.

Mrs. Dowd pursed her lips. "Uh..." She seemed to struggle to find the right words. "Mr. Caudry is, well, very particular. He's gone through several administrative assistants, I'm afraid. He's, uh, quite valuable to the firm, you understand, so we give him a certain latitude. We're hoping you'll be the right fit."

"Oh, I'll do my best," she assured the woman, feeling a disquiet in her stomach that she could not dismiss. "Uh..."

"Yes?" Mrs. Dowd looked over her spectacles at her.

"What happens if he doesn't like me? Will there be another position you can assign me to?"

The woman grimaced. "Let's cross that bridge when we come to it, shall we?"

From her expression, Emily did not feel confident that she could transfer should she fail. Suddenly, she realized she could easily lose this job she had fought so hard to land! She took a deep breath and vowed to herself she would work hard to please her apparently demanding boss.

Mrs. Dowd knocked on the oak door and listened for a moment. When she heard no answer, she opened it and peeked in. When she pulled back, Emily thought she seemed relieved. "Mr. Caudry appears to be out for the moment. I'll leave it to you to introduce yourself when he returns."

The woman left quickly as if afraid to be around when Mr. Caudry returned, her heels clicking softly once she reached the linoleum of the cubicle farm. Emily stood and surveyed her domain, her mouth half-open in shock. Her area was about eight feet wide by six feet deep, partially hidden from the lowly workers beyond by a four-foot-tall panel of dark wood that covered half of the entrance. A full wall separated this office from the one next to it. A tall filing cabinet stood against it. Her small desk sat just to the right of his door. A computer and phone were the only two items on it.

She wondered if this alleged ogre Mr. Caudry would allow her to place a small plant or a picture there. Emily sat down and swiveled the chair smoothly under her. Looking up, she noted how the paneling nearly hid her from the view of the cubicles. That made her smile. Emily vowed she would be the best damn secretary she could be. She felt she'd died and gone to heaven.

She needed this break. Her life had seemed to lurch from one crisis to another. Growing up in Kansas City, she never imagined she'd be in this position at age twenty-nine. Her life was supposed to have worked out by now. When she was a child, her father had been the center of her world—strong, handsome, caring—and very definitely the "man of the house." He had been ten years older than her mother and she had loved him so deeply, Emily wanted to have that kind of relationship with a man when she was older. He protected the family and took care of things. And yes, her mother did dote on him. Perhaps that attitude would be considered old-fashioned now, she mused, but it worked for them.

When Emily went away to college she wasn't really sure about what kind of career she wanted. It was an adventure to her—her first step toward a new life that she expected would mirror her mother's, who had met her true love right after she graduated. There was no conscious thought of obtaining her "MRS degree"—Emily was far too modern for that outdated concept—but she did find herself looking at her dates as potential life mates.

Her world shattered in October of her sophomore year. Her mother called in a tearful panic—her father had died suddenly of a heart attack. Her mother was distraught and unable to cope. After Emily got over the initial shock, she packed up her belongings and returned home. For the next four years, she took care of her mother, who had gone into a grief so deep it would seem she might never come out. Emily found herself in the role of caregiver, which wasn't how she saw herself—she wanted someone to take care of her.

When her mother finally began to come out of her depression, Emily felt too much time had passed for her to return to college. She found a job as a store clerk and tried to find a life separate from her mother, although she still lived at home.

Her mother finally began to date, which pleased Emily. Of course, no man could take the place of her father. Still, it was encouraging to see her mother finding happiness again.

Emily began to date as well, but never seemed to meet the right kind of man. Most had been immature or stuck on themselves. That was, until Adam had come into her life. She met him through work. He reminded her of his father—sure of himself, as well as handsome and intelligent. His only flaw was his quick temper, but Emily felt she could change him.

She admired his forceful personality and could imagine herself being protected from a harsh world with Adam by her side. Sometimes, when faced with an annoying bill collector or petty bureaucrat, she secretly delighted having Adam to sic on them.

They soon became an exclusive couple and Emily already imagined what their house would look like and the names of their three children. At age twenty-six, she was sure her life was back on track.

Her mother announced she was going to marry her boyfriend, and Emily and Adam felt it was the perfect time to set up housekeeping together. Emily couldn't wait to start her most important job—being a mother. Though they lived together for a year, Adam kept putting off any firm dates on an engagement, let alone a marriage. Emily had gone along, thinking he just needed more time. They were together and that was what mattered.

During this time, Adam's personality began to change. His temper, which had only flared occasionally before they had moved in together, manifested itself more often. He'd yell over some minor transgression and throw something, scaring her. Almost immediately he would be contrite and promise it would never happen again. He had just been caught in a weak moment, he'd tell her.

"You know, you've been putting pressure on me to get married and I guess I just snapped," he would say, neatly shifting some of the blame to Emily.

She forgave him, of course. They were soul mates, destined to be together.

She realized something was terribly awry with her vision of them as an ideal couple when she found a pair of woman's panties in the glove box of Adam's car. They certainly weren't hers—not a bright red, frilly pair like that! She confronted him and he exploded.

"What are you doing snooping around my car?!"

It was his attempt, she realized, of turning the attention away from his transgression and back onto her. She wasn't having any of it. She waved the panties in his face and demanded to know who they belonged to and what was he doing. For the first time, she was too angry to back down. The argument did not last long—Emily found herself on the receiving end of his fist and was knocked unconscious.

When she awoke, she was lying on her bed as a shamed and sorrowful Adam tended to her, telling her how sorry he was. "You just made me so angry," he kept saying.

It was all too much. Her image of Adam as a man as good as her father had been was shattered in that moment. She didn't argue with him or tell him it was all right—she just let him babble on about how it would never happen again while she made her quiet plans.

Emily was far too embarrassed to go home to her mother and stepfather's house. Her eye had turned black by the next day when Adam went to work. "Put some makeup on that—I don't want people thinking I'm a wife-beater or something," he said, hurrying on when he saw her stunned expression. "We'll work through this, honey, I know we will."

When he was gone, Emily called the store and quit on the spot. She told them to send her final paycheck to her mother to hold for her. She phoned her mother and said she was breaking up with Adam and promised to visit her soon, but she had to get away for a while. She offered no other explanation.

Emily packed up her few meager belongings and left Kansas City behind. She headed east to St. Louis, where she planned to reinvent herself. It hadn't been easy. She had lurched from one job to another, always managing to hang on and determined not to go home and face her old life. She had to stand on her own.

Now she felt this job might be her chance to gain a foothold and start making new friends. She couldn't think about finding a new man yet—that part of her life was too painful. But at least she could prove to herself she was going to be all right. Life would go on.

So why did she feel so hollow about her decision? Emily couldn't help wonder what happened to the men like her father, who were strong and compassionate and not at all abusive.

Emily shook her head as if to clear out the old bad memories. She ran her hands along the smooth dark wood of her desk, smelling the fresh polish. Opening a few drawers, she noted they were all empty. Supplies, she thought—I must get supplies.

She had fetched some paperclips, pens, paper and a stapler from the office supply cabinet and was trying to remember how to sign into the computer system when a man strode into her area. Emily sat bolt upright, not sure if this man was Mr. Caudry or a client. He was tall, with dark hair and a sharp nose. She pegged his age at somewhere in his late thirties or early forties—far too young to match the image Mrs. Dowd had created in her mind. His lips were pressed together as if in disappointment. His eyes seemed to pierce her to her soul and in that moment, Emily knew he must be her new boss.

"Mr., uh, Caudry?" she squeaked.

"Yes? Who are you?"

"I'm Emily Robinson, your new administrative assistant. Mrs. Dowd—"

"I see," he said dismissively, shaking his head. "She just keeps trying, doesn't she?" His voice was calm and steady and it resonated deep within her. "You should know, I hate that politically correct term, 'administrative assistant.' There's nothing wrong with being called a secretary."

Emily felt a stab of fear and fought to overcome it. "Oh no, sir! That'll be fine. I promise to serve you in whatever way you need, Mr. Caudry," she began and stopped when he waved his hand, cutting her off.

"Yes, that's what they all say, at first. Your predecessor lasted a month before I fired her. The one before that quit after two months." He paused and looked over his shoulder at the cubicles. "I'll bet they have a pool going on how long you last."

"If you could tell me, please, what they did wrong, perhaps—"

"What they did wrong, Miss Robinson, is they did not apply themselves." He paused. "It *is* Miss Robinson, isn't it?"

She nodded.

"I suppose it wasn't all their fault," he continued, "apparently they no longer teach English in our schools. They came in here with the attitude that poor grammar and spelling and generally sloppy work is sufficient."

Emily's mouth worked but no sound came out. Finally, she managed, "Well, I've always been good in English—"

"Yes, that's what two of the last five secretaries told me. It didn't seem to help." He brushed past her and went into his office, shutting the door firmly behind him. Emily let out a breath. Her face was hot and she felt a sheen of sweat all over her body. She grabbed a tissue and blotted her face quickly, trying to regain her composure.

She didn't understand why he seemed to have taken such a sudden dislike to her. Emily knew she looked good—she was fit and trim and people always told her she was attractive, with long light brown hair and a dazzling smile. So what was his problem?

The phone buzzed. She panicked for a moment when she realized it was Mr. Caudry. She found the right button and said, "Yes, Mr. Caudry?"

"Bring me a cup of coffee, please. No cream and just one-half packet of sugar."

"Uhh, right away, Mr. Caudry." She had almost questioned him. Secretaries didn't get coffee anymore, did they? But it was her first day and frankly, she felt happy to fulfill his request in order to please him. Emily jumped up and went to the employee lounge and poured coffee into a Styrofoam cup. She carefully added exactly one-half packet of sugar and stirred. As she was about to leave, pleased with herself, another woman came in, a pretty blonde with her hair up in a bun. She caught sight of the cup and asked, "Are you the one?"

"Pardon me?"

"The new secretary? For Caustic Caudry?"

The office nickname for her new boss didn't do anything for her confidence. "Uh, yes, I am."

"I'm Heather."

"Oh, I'm Emily. Nice to meet you."

"Word of advice?"

"Uh, sure."

"Mr. Caudry hates those Styrofoam cups." She went to the cupboard and pulled out a clean mug with the company logo on the side. "Use one of these."

Emily flushed with gratitude for Heather. "Oh! Thank you! I don't want to make a bad first impression." She poured the coffee into the mug.

"Trust me, with that man, no one can make a good first impression. Just ride it out as long as you can." She shook her head and turned and headed for the refrigerator.

Emily, feeling shaken by her close call, went back to the office and knocked on the door. "Mr. Caudry?" she said softly. "Mr. Caudry?"

"Come in, damn it!"

She hurried inside, holding up the cup. She noticed at once that his desk was completely clear of any clutter. "I'm sorry,

Mr. Caudry, I don't yet know how you want to be disturbed. Do you prefer I use the intercom or knock or just come in?"

For the first time, Caudry paused, his eyes seeming to soften. "Well, that's nice of you to ask. When I've asked you to get me coffee, you may knock once and come in. Place the coffee on my desk and leave immediately. I'm often on the phone and I won't want to be bothered."

"Yes, Mr. Caudry." She placed his coffee within reach and left at once, pleased that she had some kind of small breakthrough. Maybe this won't be so bad after all, she thought.

If she had only known.

CHAPTER TWO

Emily quickly learned that nearly everything was a test. Pass and he'd nod his acceptance; fail and he'd express his great disappointment in that maddeningly calm voice of his. She knew she could be fired at any time and vowed to learn from her mistakes. She needed this job!

She was called in to dictate a letter and Emily was so nervous she could hardly sit still. She tried to remember her shorthand, but her boss spoke so quickly! When she left, three pages of notes in hand, she despaired to get it right.

Taking a deep breath, she started right away, hoping she could remember what her notes missed. She spent a half-hour typing it up on her computer until Mr. Caudry buzzed her and asked, "What's taking so long? I could've written it myself by now!"

Emily wondered about that too—wouldn't it be easier for him to simply write up the damn letters himself? Isn't that what computers are for? "I'll be right in, sir."

She printed out the two-page letter, rose on shaky legs, knocked once on his door and went in. She passed the letter over quietly and waited. It didn't take him long to scan it.

"What is this? I didn't say 'take'—I clearly said 'make.' Where did you learn shorthand, anyway?"

"I'm sorry, Mr. Caudry, I can fix it."

He found two more mistakes—all in all, not bad, considering, she thought. They were easily fixable. A normal boss would've simply asked her to redo it and let it go.

But not Mr. Caudry.

"This is unacceptable, completely unacceptable. I can see I'm going to have to talk to Mrs. Dowd." His voice was calm, just like before, which made her feel worse. She almost would've preferred he yelled at her. But to be admonished by that calm, forceful voice made her feel like a misbehaving child, not a grown woman!

Emily stood there and took it, her eyes downcast. Her heart beat wildly and she felt she was about to lose her job—and for no good reason! She was trying to learn! Just give her a little time!

"Please, sir," she blurted. "I promise to do better. It's only my first day!"

He took a long slow breath. "Very well," he said. "I hope you learn quickly. As you've probably discovered, I have limited patience with errors."

Emily corrected the mistakes and vowed not to make any others. But there were so many letters he demanded! He was still young—it didn't make sense for him to be so technically inept with his computer.

Over the next two days, whether by nervousness or carelessness, Emily gave him two more letters with mistakes on them. To most bosses, it would've simply been first week adjustments, but Mr. Caudry was not like most bosses.

"I'm sorry," he told her Wednesday, holding her latest letter with two red circles around the typos, "but this isn't working out. I can't conduct my business when I have to constantly be correcting your typing errors."

"I'm so sorry, Mr. Caudry, please give me another chance! It's all so new and—"

"Grammar is new? Spelling is new?"

She felt her face grow hot. "Un, no, I didn't mean that. It's just that this is only my third day. I'm trying really hard—"

"If you were trying hard, you wouldn't be making these silly errors." His voice was calm, as usual. "I'm afraid I'm going to have to call Mrs. Dowd and ask to have you replaced with someone whose English skills are more solid."

Emily could not face going back out on the job market so soon. "Please, Mr. Caudry! I'll do anything to keep this job! Anything!"

He paused for a long time. She finally glanced up and saw his expression. His head was tipped to one side and he was studying her, like a scientist might mull a thorny problem. She waited breathlessly for him to speak.

"There was one secretary who almost made it," he said at last, wistfulness in his voice. Emily waited, certain she could learn something valuable. "She made mistakes at first, just like you. She also begged for a second and a third chance. She told me she would rather be punished than be fired. It seemed to work for a while."

"P-punished?" What the hell did that mean? Dock her pay?

"Yes. Since she was acting like a child, I treated her as a child. Perhaps that might work for you."

She looked up, confused. "Uh, well..."

"Or we can end it right here." He picked up the phone. "I can ask Mrs. Dowd to replace you. Just tell her it didn't work out and that you'll be leaving immediately."

She shook her head. "I'm sorry, sir. Please don't call her." She had too many debts to start over now! If she left, she'd lose her apartment for sure. "I'll do anything to help me learn more quickly," she repeated.

He nodded. After a long minute, he put down the phone. "Very well." He placed the letter in the middle of the blotter, the two pages side by side, and turned them around so she could read them. She could see the two red marks indicating her mistakes.

"I want you to lean over the desk on your elbows," he said. "Put your face down close to your work."

Confused, Emily did as she was told, feeling a thrum throughout her body. She knew this wasn't right, and yet... something was happening to her. Something she couldn't explain.

"No, closer," he said.

She scooted up until her thighs bumped against the desk and her face was less than a foot from the papers. She realized she was in a very vulnerable position. Emily could feel sweat begin to collect on her upper lip and neck.

Mr. Caudry gave her a moment to study her unacceptable work. Then, with deliberate slowness, he opened the desk drawer and pulled out a thick wooden ruler. Emily's eyes widened and she fought a gasp that bubbled up from within. He held the ruler in his hands for a moment, giving her time to understand her predicament. Slowly, he walked around behind her. That thrumming feeling in her stomach expanded, moving to her loins and breasts and she tried not to shiver from anticipation.

"The rule we came up with, that secretary and I, was one stroke for each mistake, at first. Later mistakes required increasing the number of strokes per incident. It did wonders for her concentration. She reduced her errors almost immediately."

Emily couldn't believe it. He was going to spank her!? That sort of thing wasn't allowed in the workplace! She could sue! She flashed back to a time when she had been nine or ten and her father had spanked her for some transgression. He had wrapped his left arm around her upper body to hold her in place and gave her five quick swats on her bottom through her skirt. She had cried, but it had also made her feel funny inside.

"Mr. Caudry..." she began.

"Of course, it would be far easier just to replace you. After all, this requires a certain amount of work on my part—time I could be spending selling. Did you know I'm the company's number one salesman?"

"Y-yessir," she squeaked.

"So I leave it to you. If you'd like to be trained to be a better secretary, fine. But if you find this too demeaning or objectionable, then you may get up right now and go. I'll let Mrs. Dowd know."

Emily's mind raced. How could this be happening to her? This was the twenty-first century! A voice in her head declared:

Bosses can't treat their employees this way!

But another part of her, deep down inside, told her something quite different—something startling and naughty.

This is extremely arousing.

She squeezed her legs together and realized it was true. It had been true when her father had spanked her and it was still true today. That strange feeling began to bubble up inside her and her pussy grew moist.

"Sir," she finally said, not sure which voice was about to speak, the modern woman or that other voice, the dark one. She felt she could've gone either way. "Sir, please teach me to be a better secretary."

Emily's knees grew weak when she realized what she'd just said—and why she had said it. She needed it. It wasn't as much for Mr. Caudry as it was for her.

"Very well. You made two mistakes today and one yesterday. That's three swats with this ruler. It would be best if you didn't make any noise." He went to a cabinet and turned on a radio. Jazz music filled the air. Emily braced herself. She didn't dare look back. Instead, she kept her eyes on her mistakes.

Whack!

The first blow was a shock, but it was tolerable. Only afterward did she feel the burn of the mark on her flesh, through her clothes. She couldn't help herself, she wiggled her behind, trying to cool the fire. He made no comment.

Whack!

This blow was harder. She bit her lip to keep from crying out. Emily had a sudden image of herself, hunched over his desk, her brown hair in disarray, her ass wiggling at him. She felt embarrassment mix in with arousal in her stomach and loins.

Whack!

The pain was sharp, but she immediately felt better now that it was over. She shook her bottom from side to side, not caring that he was staring at it. She just had to cool it off! The pain softened and spread and Emily realized with great embarrassment it was making her wetter! She pressed her thighs together and hoped he wouldn't notice.

He came around the desk and put the ruler away. "Very well. You accepted your punishment with grace. You may pick up the letter and go make your corrections."

Emily straightened up at once, grabbed the letter and fled. Closing the door behind her, she looked out over the cubicles, certain that everyone would be staring at her. But the office seemed to hum along normally. No one paid her any attention. She ducked down behind her partition and sat gingerly in her chair, wincing at the slight sting. Yet she could not deny the feeling it had given her. Her clit seemed to be buzzing. She wanted to press her fingers against it and come. Debating whether she should correct the letter or make a quick trip to the bathroom, she paused. What would Mr. Caudry want? She made the corrections instead.

She took the freshly printed letter into his office and placed it on the desk. Her insides churned and she hoped she hadn't missed any more errors! At long last, Mr. Caudry nodded and gave her a thin smile.

"See how quickly you learned?"

"Thank you, Mr. Caudry," she said and began to back out of the room.

"But you forgot one thing," he said, freezing her in her tracks.

"W-w-what, sir?"

He held up the letter. "How am I supposed to get this to the recipient?"

She felt a sudden pang of fear. She had forgotten to type up the envelope! How stupid! "Oh! I'm sorry! I'll get you the envelope at once!"

He nodded. She fled.

Emily fed an envelope into the printer and typed out the address, not bothering to sit down. Her body seemed to be on fire, wondering if he would spank her again. It felt strange—part of her was terrified by the idea and another part of her was secretly thrilled by it. Why? Shaking her head, she took the envelope into Mr. Caudry's office.

"Here you go, sir. I'm sorr—"

"Assume the position."

She stared at him, stricken. "Sir?"

"Did you not want to keep your job?"

"Uh, no sir, I mean, yes, sir," she said and quickly moved up against the desk, bracing herself with her elbows. Her heart pounded and her pussy throbbed.

"That's going to be two strokes this time," he informed her, sliding open the drawer and taking out that damned ruler.

He did not waste time. Whack! Whack! It was suddenly over. Emily stayed in position until he gave her permission to rise. When she did, her face red and her body trembling, he gave her another smile. It made her shiver with fear or desire, she couldn't tell which.

"I'm glad to see that you are learning so quickly. There's hope for you yet, Miss Robinson."

"Yes, sir. Thank you, sir." She retreated.

Outside, she paused long enough to grab her purse and headed for the bathroom. Safely inside a stall, she pulled her pantyhose down and flipped up her skirt, twisting back to examine her bottom. Each mark with the ruler was clearly outlined—five in all. Three on her left cheek, two on her right.

Now that she was alone, Emily couldn't stop herself. She sat on the toilet and her hand went between her legs without even thinking about it. Her pussy was dripping wet, as if she had undergone an hour of foreplay instead of a painful spanking. Touching her clit made her shudder with pleasure. Biting her lip to keep from moaning aloud, Emily rubbed herself to a quick climax, right there in the bathroom. It was something she had never done before in the workplace.

What is wrong with me? she wondered.

When she returned to her desk, she realized a precedent had been established. Is that what she wanted? Or should she quit despite her shaky financial situation? Something besides her need for money made her decide to stick it out a while longer. Just to see where this all would lead. Maybe, just maybe, she'd learn so quickly the spankings would stop and she and Mr. Caudry would be able to achieve some kind of détente.

But her pussy told her a different story.

***

That night, after a half-bottle of wine, Emily was relaxing on the couch in her sweatpants and T-shirt, glad to have ditched her confining work clothes. She recalled her embarrassing punishment and tried to understand her feelings about it. Everything she had learned told her that this was wrong. She shouldn't be allowing this behavior. No job was worth it!

Why, I'm going to march right into Mrs. Dowd's office tomorrow and let her know what's going on! I won't put up with this kind of treatment! What kind a man is this Mr. Caudry?

Her clit throbbed and Emily's internal diatribe faded away. Her hand stole to the vee of her legs and rubbed her pussy through the soft material. Her eyes closed and her head tipped back.

"Ohhhhh," she breathed.

Her fingers wiggled their way underneath the waistband and into her panties. Her pussy was once again wet and she shook her head. *Stop this!* She scolded herself. *You're not supposed to be turned on by that kind of behavior!* But her fingers ignored her. They drew up the moisture to her clit, which seemed swollen with desire.

"Oh, god," she moaned, rubbing herself. Her climax was right there, hovering and she brought it crashing over her in less than a minute. Her fingers kept moving.

"Jesus!" She muttered when she had recovered and felt another one coming along. "What is happening to me?"

CHAPTER THREE

For the rest of the week, Emily double- and triple-checked her work, handing over perfect letters, complete with envelopes, for Mr. Caudry's approval. She even remembered to run them through the meter for him. She never gave him a reason to punish her and, in return, she received his thin smile, which she had come to learn was his only sign of appreciation. But it was clear he did appreciate her efforts. Emily felt a breakthrough had been achieved and she was certain she would succeed where the others had failed.

Yet something else was happening to her as well. Her body rebelled at her perfection. What was that all about? Was she trying to get into trouble? Her fingers seemed clumsy when she typed and her eyesight faltered when she proof-read her work. It was on Friday that her fingers typed a "u" where an "o" should've been in a client's name and, for some odd reason, her eyes missed it. She took the letter into his office and set it on his desk, along with the envelope. She smiled and he nodded back, his face expressionless. She turned and left him there and returned to her desk, humming softly.

The intercom buzzed. Her heart froze.

"Miss Robinson?"

"Yes, Mr. Caudry?"

"I need you."

With a sense of impending doom, Emily stepped into his office and closed the door. He was holding the letter up and asked simply: "What is our client's name?"

"Uh, Mr. Dardon, sir."

"Spell it."

"Uh, D-A-R-D-O-N." Emily thought she might fall through the floor.

"Then why did you spell it D-A-R-D-U-N?"

Her hand went to her mouth and she stared at him. "I'm sorry, sir—"

"You remember the rules?"

"Yes, yes, sir." She went at once to the front of his immaculate desk and leaned over onto her elbows, her hair hanging over the egregious letter. She could see the red pen mark where he had circled the client's name. How could she have missed that?

"That's three strokes for the letter..." he paused dramatically. "And another three for the envelope." He tossed it next to the letter and Emily could see she had made the same mistake. A low moan escaped from her throat.

Mr. Caudry removed the ruler, giving her time to see it. He moved out of her range of vision and she heard the radio being turned on. She closed her eyes and waited.

The first two blows landed and her bottom stung. She bit her lip hard to keep from crying out. Then the heat began to spread and she knew her clit was at full attention, just like that.

Whack! Whack!

"Ohhhhh," she groaned, wigging her bottom, trying to cool herself off.

"Shhhh," he admonished and she sucked in her breath.

When he completed the last two strokes, her head dropped down to the blotter and tears fell from her eyes. Mr. Caudry stood silently behind her. When she could compose herself, she lifted up to see that her tears had stained the letter. She gathered it up, along with the envelope, and turned to face her demanding employer.

"Please, sir, may I go make those corrections now?"

He nodded, eyes watching her.

She took a deep breath and, with as much dignity as she could muster, left his office. She dropped the materials on her desk and went at once to the bathroom. Examining her reddened bottom in the stall, she wondered how she could've made such a stupid mistake? She knew the client's name, damn it!

Emily sat on the toilet and winced when her sore ass touched the seat. Her hand went at once to her clit and she brought herself to a quick orgasm. After coming down from the release, she took her time with the next one. When she finally was able to stand and get dressed, she tried to chide herself for her actions, but that voice inside her said: *Shut up— you know you wanted it. You don't really think that typo was an accident, do you?*

Of course it was, she tried to tell herself.

Back at her desk, she fixed the mistakes and brought them into Mr. Caudry.

"About time," he said, but his voice was light.

She felt a sudden chill—did he know what she did in the bathroom? No, of course not, she assured herself. How could he?

"Sorry, sir."

Back in her chair, she wondered about her incredible deference to this man. She regularly called him "Sir"! He hadn't demanded that—she doubted it was legal anyway. Yet here she was, calling him "sir" all the time! She shook her head. This was by far the strangest job she'd ever had. She made a mental note to start spreading her resume around. It might be a good idea to get out of there!

***

That night Emily tried to make sense of what was happening to her. It was all so confusing! She felt like she was being too naïve and yet, there was something she clearly liked about it. God! What would her mother say!

The phone rang and she answered it. "Hello?"

"Hey, Emily, what's up?"

"Oh, hi, Julie. Nothing." Julie was a friend she'd met at her last job.

"How's the job going?"

"Uh, good." Emily was not ready to tell her about her strange boss.

"Good. You feel like going out? It's Friday. Maybe we could troll the bars for single men!"

That suddenly sounded just like what she needed. To get out of this apartment and stop worrying about her stupid job! "That sounds great! Wanna meet somewhere?"

"Nah, let me come over, then we'll only have to take one car. Save the environment and all that."

"Sure."

Emily put on her "go-to" dress, a shiny black number with spaghetti straps. It usually made all the men pay attention. She had on a black strapless bra and matching panties underneath. She fixed her makeup, rouging her lips and adding eyeliner, giving her a sexier look that the conservative image she tried to portray at work. In the mirror, she saw an appealing young woman staring back at her and winked. "Maybe you'll get lucky tonight," she cooed and laughed.

Julie came by within a half-hour and they hugged each other. Julie was a taller redhead with a figure she kept in shape with hours of work in the gym. Men loved her, but Julie was very particular. Tonight she had on a form-fitting green dress that went perfectly with her red hair. "I'm so happy to see you again, girl! I was worried that you might have to go home to mamma!"

"I just about did! I was broke, you know."

"I know. It's awful being broke. Have you gotten paid yet?"

"No, not until next week. But I don't care! I'm going to have some fun tonight anyway!"

"Glad to hear. But don't worry. The way we're dressed, we probably won't have to buy a drink all night!"

Julie drove to a hot spot that they both liked, Rosie's Bar & Grill. The place had a live band on weekends and many of the local singles hung out, cruising for action or just enjoying their friends. Julie had been right—Emily had to buy exactly one beer during the evening. They danced, they drank and they partied away the workweek with some serious fun.

Neither one found "Mr. Right" that night. Not even "Mr. Maybe." The men seemed too drunk, too stuck on themselves or too arrogant for either of their tastes. They wound up going home alone back to Emily's apartment shortly after midnight.

"Come on in, I'll fix you a drink."

"Ohh, you tryin' to seduce me, girl?"

"Oh, stop! I'm not that kind of girl!" Emily teased back.

"Tell ya the truth, I could really use a cup of coffee. I probably shouldn't be driving."

"No problem. Coming right up. Decaf, right?"

"Right. I don't wanna be up all night. I just want to get home before the cops find out I'm on the road."

Emily busied herself in the kitchen. Julie came in and sat at the small table. "Hey, you never told me about your job! What are you doing now, anyway?"

Emily felt a pang of something go through her. Was it embarrassment? Fear? She shook her head. "Oh, I'm just a secretary to some salesman at Bonham Industries. No big deal."

"Really? That's too bad."

"What do you mean?"

"Well, I think you should have a job you like. Take mine, for example. I love working at the art gallery. Pay's not too great, but I meet such interesting people."

"You mean rich people, right?"

"Yeah, rich people." She smiled. "Hey, maybe one of them will come in and sweep me off my feet!"

"You'd do that? Fall for a guy just for the money?"

Julie stared at her and shook her head. "Emily, wake up! This is the twenty-first century! No one marries for love anymore."

"I want to. Maybe I'm old-fashioned, but I still want love." She poured two cups of coffee and set one in front of her friend.

"Aww, isn't that sweet. We are the same age, aren't we? Then why do I have sooo much more maturity than you?"

"Oh, crap, you were always a cynic. It has nothing to do with maturity."

"Hey, being cynical has saved me from many a bad relationship!"

Emily tipped her head. "Yeah, yeah. Do I need remind you of Brian again!" Brian had been Julie's last "true love." It had ended badly, like all the others.

"At least he was rich!" Julie took a sip. "Okay, tell me something good about your job. Something you like."

"Uh, well..." She couldn't say anything about how Mr. Caudry treated her. It was far too embarrassing! "Let's see...my boss is kinda strict."

"That's not something to like!"

"I know. I was just thinking out loud. Let's see, something I like..."

"Wait, how strict is he? Is he anything like Bob?"

Emily opened her mouth in shock. Bob had been their boss, when they worked together at a big office before Julie quit to take the art gallery job and Emily had been laid off. But that man wasn't at all like Mr. Caudry. Bob was a stern taskmaster, yes, but there was absolutely nothing sexy about him. Suddenly she stopped and realized she had just admitted to herself that Mr. Caudry was sexy!

"Hey, what's that expression all about? He *is* like Bob, isn't he?"

"No, no. Not at all. Bob was a jerk, a man who hated people. Mr. Caudry's not like that at all."

"You call him Mr. Caudry? Not 'Joe' or 'Sam' or whatever his name is?"

"Uh, no. I don't even know what his first name is. Besides, it's only my first week." And what a week it had been!

"Well, he sounds liked a stuffed shirt. Is he cute at least?"

That question caught her off guard. "Uh, well, I don't, uh..."

"Ha! You think he's cute! Ohh, I can see it now, Mr. and Mrs. Alphonse Caudry!" She giggled.

"Alphonse? You think his name is Alphonse?"

"It could be. Come on, tell me what he looks like. Let me hear about your future husband!"

Emily could not imagine them together. "Stop that! Ewww! Like I said, he's stern. I mean, I wouldn't call him ugly or anything, but I wouldn't call him cute, not by a long shot! He's kinda tall, with dark hair."

"Does he like you?"

"I don't know. I guess. He sure doesn't like mistakes!"

"Oh? What does he do? Spank you?" She giggled.

Emily took a big sip of her coffee to hide her shock and choked on it. "Stop it!" she sputtered. "That's not even funny."

"Well, excuse me, dear. I thought it was hilarious."

"You're still drunk."

"Yeah, well, you still haven't told me much. Sounds like your job is kinda boring."

"Yeah, it's boring." Emily thought it was time to change the subject. "So tell me about the gallery? What new perversions are you displaying this week?"

Julie laughed. "You're still going on about those paintings by Langston? I thought they were sexy! I just about wore out my vibrator during his show!"

Emily had thought they had been highly erotic as well, but she had pretended to be shocked by them. Perhaps it was to uphold her image as "the good girl" in comparison to Julie, who was always a bit wild. Truth be told, Emily had dropped by Julie's gallery a lot during those weeks and had many of her own very satisfying orgasms at home alone after each visit.

"You always were the slutty one," she teased her friend.

"Yeah, well, better than being boring!" She finished her coffee and looked at her watch. "Oh! It's late. I've got to get up and open the gallery tomorrow. I'd better go."

"Hey, thanks for taking me out. I needed some cheering up."

"Don't worry about your job. It will get better."

"I'm thinking of sending my resume out, just in case this doesn't work out."

"Why? You think your mean boss will fire you?"

"He's pretty particular. He's gone through, like, a dozen secretaries already. I live in fear that I'll do something wrong and he'll send me packing."

"Take my advice. Flirt with him a little. Don't look at me like that—I'm not saying throw yourself at him! Just be nice. You know what I'm talking about. Most men respond to that kind of thing. He may decide you're worth keeping around."

Emily nodded, thinking, *If she only knew!* She was already giving him exactly what he wanted. Her fear was, how much more would he want?

CHAPTER FOUR

Monday morning, Emily was determined to put a stop to this behavior she had allowed herself to fall into. It just wasn't right. When Mr. Caudry arrived and nodded at her before disappearing into his office, she steeled herself and gently knocked on the door.

"Yes?"

She opened it and peeked in.

"Get me a cup of coffee," he barked before she could speak.

"Uh, yes, sir." She retreated, cursing herself. Why was she so timid around him? Meekly, she retreated to the break room and poured him a cup in a fresh mug. She added one-half packet of sugar, just as he liked, and returned to the office. She knocked on the door and entered.

"Fine, put it down there." He was reading through the morning paper.

She did and waited.

He looked up. "What?"

"Sir..." Emily began. Her voice failed her as he continued to stare at her, his patience clearly being tested.

"Well? Spit it out. I haven't got all day."

"Sir," she tried again. "About last week..."

He waited and she forged ahead.

"That was, uh, inappropriate behavior for the workplace. Surely you know that. I mean..."

His gaze disrupted her thoughts. "As I recall, you seemed to prefer it to being replaced, did you not?"

"Well, yes, sir..."

"I gave you the option. I didn't think you were working out. I went out of my way to suggest something another secretary had done in order to remain employed. If you want to change your mind, fine. There's the door. I'll inform Mrs. Dowd."

"I want to keep my job!" Emily blurted. "It's just that, uh, I don't think Mrs. Dowd would approve of, uh, our behavior last week. It's not proper conduct."

"I decide what's proper here. Not you and not Mrs. Dowd."

"But it's against all—"

"I'm not going to argue with you. If you no longer want to trade punishments in lieu of being fired, so be it. Just don't make any more mistakes." He snapped the paper up and began to read.

Feeling dismissed, Emily found herself nodding, almost bowing, as she retreated. Mr. Caudry didn't even look up from his paper.

Outside, she felt a little better. Didn't she? Then why did her body feel so let down? She tried to dismiss those feelings and concentrated on her work. An hour later, Mr. Caudry buzzed her to take another letter. She cringed to herself. She knew she'd better get it right!

"Very well, Mr. Caudry."

She gathered her pad and pen and went into his office. Her knees were shaking as she sat across from his desk and readied her pen. Caudry had a report open in front of him and he didn't look up as he began citing from it during his dictation of the letter. Emily did her very best to keep up, but some of the terms were confusing.

"Excuse me," she interrupted at one point. "What was that term? Mandrel?"

He seemed annoyed, but he answered her anyway. "Yes, it's an object used to shape machined work. If you want to work here, you'd better get used to these terms."

"Yes, sir. I'm sorry, sir. Uh, is it spelled with an 'e' or an 'i'?"

"E," he said. "Can we continue now?"

"Of course. Sorry."

He went on and her hand scribbled in response. He threw out terms that she'd only vaguely heard of, such as "lathe dog," "direct metal deposition" and "collette." She didn't know what they were, and she didn't dare interrupt him again. She vowed to look them up as soon as she could.

When she was dismissed, she had four pages of notes that he wanted collapsed into a two-page letter. She sat at her computer and despaired getting it right. Why was he so short with her? Hadn't she done everything he had asked?

She remembered Julie's advise to flirt with him a little. He didn't seem to be the type that responded to flirting. Did he have a wife, kids? She doubted it. And if he didn't, what did he do at night? Watch videos of women being spanked?

She giggled suddenly. She bet he did!

Emily typed up the letter, checking it carefully for typos and other mistakes. Just to make sure, she checked it again before she knocked on his door.

"Come in."

"Here's that letter you asked for, Mr. Caudry," she said, trying to sound friendly. Maybe not flirting-friendly, but friendly nonetheless.

He nodded and took it. She turned to go.

"Miss Robinson."

She froze. Turning slowly, she saw him holding up the letter, his head shaking sadly from side to side. "Do you know what a collet is?"

"Uh, no."

"It's a type of chuck that's used to hold work in a lathe," he said. "And it's spelled, C-O-L-L-E-T, without the extra T-E you've added here."

Emily tried to ignore the roaring in her head. "Uh, well, that's a common mistake, I'm sure. I'll just fix it right away and—"

"No, I'm afraid that's not good enough. I'm sorry, Ms. Robinson, but I can't have a secretary that doesn't know the spellings of the very tools we sell."

"But it's a very simple fix, Mr. Cau—"

"Like I said, I demand perfection. And since you don't want to be subjected to any punishments, you leave me no choice." He picked up the phone and punched an extension. "Mrs. Dowd? Caudry here. I'm sorry, but I don't think Miss Robinson—"

"Wait!" The thrumming in her body was louder now.

Caudry's eyes locked onto hers. "Yes?" He put his hand over the phone.

"Okay! I'll accept your punishments! Just don't fire me, please!"

"Very well." Into the phone, he said, "Sorry, Mrs. Dowd, but I think maybe I can work this out on my own. I'll let you know if I have any further trouble."

He hung up. "Assume the position."

Meekly, Emily went to his desk and propped herself up on her elbows. The letter was in position and she could see where he'd circled "collette." It was such a simple mistake! Anyone could've made it. And then, in that moment, she knew. Everything became clear. It had nothing to do with her mistakes and everything to do with her submission to his will. Emily realized something very important. If she could endure his little fetish, she might go far in this company, maybe even get a raise. Consider this a form of flirting, she told herself.

And that darker part of herself seemed to sigh in satisfaction. Emily felt her pussy begin to throb in anticipation.

Mr. Caudry went behind her and she braced herself for her punishment. The radio went on and lively jazz music filled the room.

"Let's see, we're up to four swats per mistake, aren't we?"

"Y-yes, sir."

Suddenly, he flipped her skirt up, exposing her pantyhose to him.

"Mr. Caudry!" She jumped up and turned around, pushing her skirt back down with both hands. Her stomach felt funny and her pussy grew wet.

"This is part of the progression, my dear. If you have not learned to produce flawless work after three strokes per mistake, then simple swats alone are clearly insufficient."

"But I'm...You can't..."

Mr. Caudry just waited until she stopped sputtering.

"It's entirely up to you, Mr. Robinson. But you try my patience. If you refuse to learn my way, I have no use for you."

Emily knew she should quit right then and there. Sure, she'd probably lose her apartment and have bill collectors hound her, but wouldn't that be better than what was happening to her? But that dark and naughty part of her whispered that truth into her head that she could not deny: *This little game is making you wet.*

She stared at him for a long moment before she turned around and got back into position. She said nothing when he raised her skirt—her mind was focused on her throbbing clit and weeping pussy and couldn't wait for this to be over so she could go into the ladies room and masturbate.

Whack! Whack! Both blows struck her left cheek and she jumped at the sharpness of the paint. He was hitting her directly on her pantyhose, which offered little protection. Emily wiggled her bottom and could imagine how that must look to him.

"Settle down, Miss Robinson."

Biting her lip, she steadied herself. Whack! Whack! She gasped as her right cheek now exploded into pain and her bottom again jerked around in an effort to cool off. And there was more. As she jerked, her pussy came into contact with the edge of his desk and she nearly climaxed right then and there. She pulled away and lay panting, wondering why her body was betraying her this way.

She felt her skirt being flipped back into place and she stood, her knees shaking.

"Thank me," he said. It wasn't a request.

"Th-thank you, Mr. Caudry." She gathered up the letter and left.

There was no way she could sit down, not right now. Emily glanced over into the bullpen, certain they had heard the sharp crack of the ruler against her pantyhose. Just as before, no one paid the slightest attention to her. Grabbing her purse, she went to the bathroom. She didn't bother looking at her bottom, she could only yank her pantyhose down to her thighs and rub herself to sudden and intense orgasm, one that made her knees buckle and she had to brace herself against the wall. When she calmed down, she did it again.

She'd never had orgasms this strong before, not even with Adam.

This was becoming a very strange routine by now, she realized. Get spanked and rubbing herself to one or two quick orgasms almost immediately. This was the first time she had ever done something so naughty in the workplace. What's next, she chided herself, making photocopies of her ass?

Before she pulled up her pantyhose, she glanced around behind her to see the four red marks. They seemed darker, angrier than before. She rubbed her sore flesh and shook her head. What had she gotten herself into? And why was it so hard to stop it?

Did she really want it to stop?

Standing over the sink, Emily took a damp paper towel and patted her face to cool down, staring at herself in the mirror. She saw an attractive girl staring back, with a flush to her face and her pupils slightly dilated as if she had just taken a drug. Those hormones are powerful things, she mused. This situation seemed so strange, she could hardly believe it was happening to her. And yet, here she was, falling under the spell of her stern boss.

No, wait, she decided. *I'm really falling under the spell of my own desires. Why do I like it—it's so completely wrong!* No, she thought, shaking her head. It's not so much *like* as it is *need*. What did that make her?

She returned to her desk and sat down gingerly, wincing when her sore bottom made contact. She pulled up the letter and made the corrections. When it came out of the printer, she brought the letter and envelope in to Mr. Caudry and waited nervously for him to approve them. He nodded curtly and gave her that same thin smile that she knew represented great joy to the taciturn man. Pleased, she started to leave, when he spoke, his words cutting through her soul like an icicle.

"Miss Robinson. From now on, I don't want you to wear pantyhose."

She froze, her mouth half open to protest. But it was her pussy that spoke to her, throbbing anew, causing her knees to shake. "Yes, sir," was all she said and retreated.

CHAPTER FIVE

The next morning, Emily stepped naked from the bathroom and rooted through her drawers to find the right pair of panties to wear. Nothing sexy, for she feared he might very well see them. Just thinking about it made her body tremble. She found a pair of white granny panties and slipped them on. They made her feel safe somehow, although it was a foolish notion. It would be like holding up an umbrella to protect oneself from lightning.

She dressed in a conservative skirt and blouse and walked to her car, feeling the breeze over her legs. Normally, she disliked pantyhose, but they gave her a sense of protection. Now she was being ordered not to wear them—she should've felt elated, but it only made her shudder with both fear and desire.

She arrived first, as usual, and settled in behind her desk, her legs primly closed together, and began working on the weekly report. She could see by comparison to the other salesmen, Mr. Caudry was far and away the best and therefore the most valuable of the company's senior staff. There was no way they would ever fire him, no matter what complaints she might make.

That's assuming I would ever want to make a complaint, a voice in her head said suddenly. Before she could puzzle over that odd thought, Mr. Caudry arrived. She sat up and smiled at him and wished him a good morning.

He paused by the desk and said, "Would you come into my office, please, Miss Robinson?"

She was stunned by his politeness and jumped up to follow him inside.

"Close the door."

Emily obeyed, trying to quiet the turmoil within her.

"Did you honor my request?"

She knew at once what he meant. "Uh, yes, sir."

"Turn around. Show me."

She stared at him. This was clearly over the line. She was not going to stand here and show her boss her panties! Yet her body turned and hands seemed to move by themselves down to the hem of her skirt, even as her brain told her in no uncertain terms to stop. *Tell him this isn't right. Tell him you're not that kind of woman.*

But the hem was rising now and she seemed unable to stop herself. She could feel the air on her thighs and felt a flush rise to her face. Now her hands were up near her waist, giving Mr. Caudry a view of her panties. *What is wrong with you?* she asked herself.

She heard a long sigh of disappointment and knew what he meant. Her panties did not pass muster. They were boring and unsexy.

"Those are the ugliest panties I've ever seen," he said.

She hung her head in shame and then realized how foolish she was acting. "I'm sorry, sir, you didn't say what kind. You just said not to wear pantyhose."

"Yes, that much is good. Well, I'm not going to tell you want panties to wear. But if you insist on wearing ugly ones like that, then I'll have to ask you to remove them before punishments."

Emily thought she'd been shocked before, but his words now rocked her so hard she had to drop her hem and grab the arm of a nearby chair to keep from falling down.

"Are you all right?"

"Yes, yes, I'm sorry. I was just a little dizzy there for a second."

"Yes, well…I suggest you go out at lunch and find some panties that are more appropriate for the workplace."

"Uh, yes, sir." She didn't ask what kind would be "more appropriate." She already knew.

"Very well, you're dismissed. Please get me a cup of coffee."

He said "please" again! Emily felt she had achieved a great breakthrough in their working relationship, not pausing to consider how unusual it had become. She nodded and thanked him—thanked him!—and practically ran to do his bidding.

Emily concentrated on her work, determined not to make any mistakes. She wrote up three letters that morning, all perfect. Mr. Caudry nodded his approval and said nothing else.

When her lunch break arrived, she told her boss she was leaving. When he looked up from his desk and gave her that narrow smile, she felt a glow within as if he had just given her a raise. Emily headed at once down to a department store three blocks away and began looking through the racks of panties. She wanted sexy but not too sexy, she decided. But as her fingers moved through the racks, she found herself selecting more revealing undergarments. Stopping at one point, she went through her selections and found they were all very sexy and some were nothing more than thongs!

She quickly put the thongs back and selected three pairs, one high-cut briefs, one French cut and one bikini panties. She had to put them on her credit card, for she still had not yet been paid. This expense was really unnecessary, she told herself, since she had panties at home. But none were as sexy as these! Did she secretly want to please him?

Back at the office, she tucked her purchases into a desk drawer and went back to the reports. Mr. Caudry came back from lunch a half-hour later. She waited. Sure enough, he said, "Come into my office, please."

Emily knew exactly what he wanted. She followed him, pausing only a second to retrieve her bag of underwear. Closing the door behind her, she stood there and waited for his orders.

"Show me what you bought."

She took out the briefs and held them up. They were white and plain and only slightly sexier than the grannys she had on. He tsked and frowned and she knew at once they had been a mistake. He would probably not allow her to wear them. She put them away and removed the French cut, a pale yellow pair with a lacy edge. He gave a small smile and tipped his head. They were better, his expression told her.

Finally, she pulled out the light blue bikini briefs and he nodded. "Much better. Please put them on."

"Yes, sir," she said and started to leave.

"Where are you going?"

She froze. "Uh, I was going to the ladies room..."

"No, put them on here. You can turn around. I'm sure you won't show much."

"But sir! You can't...you can't ask me..."

Mr. Caudry said nothing, he simply stared at her. Emily found herself obeying—why did she obey him so easily? Was it his voice? His expression? She turned and dropped her bag on the chair, still holding the blue panties in one hand. She reached up underneath her skirt, tugged down her grannys and stepped out of them. Moving quickly, she slipped on the sexy pair and pulled them into position, careful not to show Mr. Caudry too much of her bottom.

Her stomach flip-flopped and she felt dizzy. She managed to stand up straight. Before she could turn around to face him, she heard him say, "Let me see them."

Emily knew that was coming. Once again, she knew she should refuse. This game had gone too far. Yet here she was, lifting her skirt up and showing her ass to her boss. What was wrong with her? She looked over her shoulder to see, for the first time, a larger smile than ever before. Compared to a normal man's smile, this would be called "slight," but to Emily, it was a huge change. He was actually pleased! She felt enormously proud and the incongruity of her situation was almost lost on her.

"Good. You may go." With that, he turned back to his desk and sat down, mentally dismissing her.

Emily felt a sudden disappointment. In an instant, she had gone from elation to depression, which was crazy. Why should she be showing her boss her underwear? And why should she care that he merely acknowledged her efforts to please him? Did she expect something more?

With that last thought echoing in her mind, she left, taking her purchases and her old panties with her. Outside, she suddenly realized she was still clutching her grannys in her fist and she quickly ducked behind her desk and thrust them into her bag. Her hands shook as she put the bag away.

For the rest of the day, Emily typed carefully, fearful of making a mistake. Not because she feared a spanking or showing her panties to her boss—after all, he'd already seen them. No, it was because she couldn't predict her own actions if that occurred. It was as if her body had electricity flowing through it.

So why, then, did she make a mistake on the last letter, the one she typed up ten minutes before quitting time? Was that her subconscious at work again? Or was she just tired after a long day? And it was such a simple mistake—a comma where a period should've gone. She never caught it before she brought the letter into her boss.

"Miss Robinson?"

The mechanical voice from her intercom chilled her. She knew at once what must've happened and she couldn't believe it. She'd been so careful! Hadn't she?

She went inside and closed the door behind her. "Y-y-yes, Mr. Caudry?"

"I've found a typo." He almost seemed pleased to have caught her in an error.

"Oh! I'm sorry, sir." She hung her head. In her mind, she felt shock, but in her loins, she felt a buzzing sensation.

"You know the rules by now, Miss Robinson."

She did indeed. Emily went to his desk and propped herself up on her elbows. He placed the letter in front of her so she could see the comma circled in red ink. She closed her eyes and waited.

"We're up to five strokes now, aren't we?" She could hear him removing the ruler from the desk. She kept her eyes tightly closed.

"Yes, sir."

She felt him move around behind her and a moment later, the radio went on. She shuddered as the music washed over her. Now her skirt was being raised up and tucked under at the top. Her new panties! He was staring at her sexy new panties! Then it hit her—is this what she wanted? Why would anyone want to be punished? Or was she somehow flirting with him?

Whack! The ruler bit into her left cheek and she gasped from the shock of it. Her clit seemed on fire and she feared she might come from this punishment. That wasn't right—how could this be happening?

Whack! He was being more deliberate today, giving her time after each blow for the sensations to rock her and to anticipate the next one.

Whack! Now her right cheek was being assaulted. Her body moved forward and she felt her swollen clit bump the edge of the desk. She gasped aloud and pulled back, her mind spinning out of control.

Whack! Her clit seemed huge and all she could think about was, *I want to come! I want to come!* Yet she dare not in front of her boss! That would be horrible!

Whack! The final blow forced her forward again and she managed with the last ounce of her dignity to keep from rubbing her clit against the desk, which would surely cause her a powerful and embarrassing orgasm. But Mr. Caudry surprised her. He grabbed her hips and pushed her forward, causing her swollen clit to collide with the edge and she couldn't help herself—she rubbed her clit against the hard surface, once, twice, and she shuddered with a huge climax, right there in front of him!

"Oh!" she squeaked, trying to disguise what had happened and knowing it was hopeless. He held her hips there as her body trembled from the power of it. Finally, he let go and she sank onto the desk, her mind awhirl.

Mr. Caudry went to a cabinet and she could hear the tinkle of glasses. He returned with a small glass of brandy and held it under her nose, rousing her.

"Here," he said. "Drink this."

Gratefully, she pulled herself to her feet and sipped at the smooth liquor. Her senses returned. All at once, Emily was overwhelmed with embarrassment. She turned her head away, a red flush washing over her neck and face.

"Oh no!"

She felt his hand on her upper arm and his voice in her ear was gentle. "Not to worry, Miss Robinson, not to worry. I think you are doing an excellent job as my secretary. In fact, I'm thinking of offering you a raise as soon as your thirty-day probationary period is up."

She nodded, unable to look him in the eye. "T-thank you, s-sir." A raise? Was he bribing her? Or was he simply just pleased, as he said?

He made her take another sip of brandy and her head cleared. Her bottom, however, burned like a brand, reminding her of her embarrassing lapse. She had climaxed in front of her boss! How could she ever live that down?

She dared not look at him. "I-I'd better go."

"Yes, I'll see you tomorrow."

She paused at the door. "Would you like me to make that correction before I leave, sir?"

"That won't be necessary. Just fix it first thing in the morning."

With effort, Emily gathered up her things and left, her ass burning and her mind in turmoil.

CHAPTER SIX

At home, Emily poured herself a big glass of wine and stood in the kitchen to drink it, leaning up against the counter. Her ass burned too much to sit down. She tried to make sense of what had happened. Surely Mr. Caudry knew what he was doing when he made her come. But he had not added to her embarrassment in any way. In fact, he had been a gentleman, bringing her brandy and telling her to let the correction go until morning. It was as if she'd seen a new side of him—a kind and gentle man.

And yet, at what cost! She had had a huge orgasm right there in his office! Would he now take advantage of her? Would he start demanding sex? Emily couldn't get her mind around that. Of course that would be wrong and she should put a stop to it. And yet, she had never, in all her years, had orgasms like she'd been having in the last several days. It was as if her body were betraying her. Everything she had been raised to be seemed suddenly inside-out and upside-down. When she was naughty, she felt good and was rewarded by her boss. When she acted as a normal woman would, he seemed terse and displeased.

She took another gulp of wine and decided not to dwell on it too much. She needed the job, yes, but it had gone beyond that now. She was beginning to realize she needed more of what her body had been getting: orgasms that shook her to her very core. It was as if she had become addicted to the pleasures she'd never before experienced.

It wasn't just the orgasms, she knew. It was Mr. Caudry himself. She liked the man, for reasons she couldn't fully explain. He excited her like no other man she had ever met before. Was it so wrong to see where this might go?

She slept soundly that night, another indication that her body was telling her it was all right. If she felt so bad, why did she sleep so well? Her mind, which was abuzz with scolding opinions, didn't keep her from dropping off as soon as her head hit the pillow.

The next morning, after her shower, Emily stood naked in front of her bedroom mirror, trying to decide what to wear. Her body was thrumming and she turned this way and that, looking at her rounded breasts and hips, the sparse hair between her legs. She knew she looked good, but she had always hidden away her charms . Since losing her virginity at age seventeen, she had had four lovers total, including Adam. None had made her feel like she did in Mr. Caudry's presence. And he hadn't made love to her!

Not yet, anyway.

Would he? She tried to visualize the stern man's hands touching her breasts, her pussy. She used her own hands and shivered when she imagined his there. The marks on her ass had faded, but they were evidence of his control over her. Control—that was such a negative word. Adam had wanted to control her and it had been all wrong. Somehow when Mr. Caudry did it, everything seemed right.

"Oh, shit, get to work!" she told her reflection.

Looking through her underwear drawer, she knew at once which panties Mr. Caudry would reject—all the high cut and most of the French cut. Only the bikini panties would do and as she stood there, looking for something to wear, she realized two facts:

She was dressing to please her boss.

And she needed more underwear. Sexy underwear.

Emily found a pair of pink bikinis that fit her well and slipped them on. She wiggled her hips, enjoying how they snugged up against her pussy. Even now, her clit seemed aroused and she could feel it rub against the silky material.

Shaking her head, she quickly got dressed in another skirt and blouse. Only this time, her skirt was a dark blue wrap-around that she had never dared to wear to work and the blouse was a white silk number that showed a hint of her lacy bra underneath. She stared at her reflection and nodded. She looked damn good.

At the office, she made sure to be standing when Mr. Caudry came in. She busied herself at the cabinet, turning to greet him as if it had been an accident. He flashed her a thin smile and nodded. "Good morning, Miss Robinson. Come into my office, please."

She followed him inside, her nerves ajangle.

"Let's see them."

Just like that? No preamble? She found herself obeying again. She started to turn around, but Mr. Caudry stopped her. "No. Face me."

That familiar flush crept up her neck and Emily felt her mouth go dry.

"Mr. Caudry!" she said.

He said nothing. He simply waited.

His power overcame her embarrassment. She licked her lips and her fingers reached down to her hem and began to pull it up. Her knees shook. His eyes were on her now and there was nowhere to hide.

Why am I doing this? she asked herself. There was no answer to that except the obvious one—she liked it, even as it scared her.

As her panties came into view, she felt her face grow redder. His eyes ate her up and she stood there, skirt up to her waist, revealing far too much to her boss.

"Very good," he said and gave her a smile. And just as suddenly, she was dismissed. He sat down and turned to his computer.

She left, feeling oddly rejected. It didn't make sense. She had been made to show her panties to her boss and afterwards, instead of feeling violated or harassed, she felt let down because he had dismissed her so quickly.

What else did she want him to do?

The possible answers to that made her shiver. She could almost feel his hands on her. Was she really falling for this strange man? She focused on the computer and got to work. As the day moved on and Emily churned out a steady stream of reports and letters, she realized just how much control she still had. On the surface, it seemed as if Mr. Caudry was treating her like his puppet, but if she never made another mistake, nothing would happen. She had the ultimate control.

But the mistakes she had made recently were silly ones, clearly due to carelessness. Or was something else going on? She decided to try an experiment. For the rest of the week, she would make no mistakes. Let's see where this goes, she told herself.

Her grand experiment lasted exactly five hours. Right after lunch, she was called into his office. Emily couldn't imagine that she'd made a mistake! She'd been so careful!

"Mrs. Dowd tells me that the report you turned in on Friday contained some errors," he informed her when she was standing nervously in front of his desk.

Oh shit, she thought. *My grand plan is being betrayed by old work!*

"Uh, really? I don't recall—"

"Let me show you," he said, placing the reports on his blotter, turned so she could see them. She knew at once what that meant. She leaned over and rested on her elbows, her ass up. Studying the report, she couldn't see anything wrong. There were no red marks on either page!

"But sir!" she said, even as she heard him turn on the radio and felt him lift up her skirt and tuck it into place. "There's nothing here!"

"Check out the column one from the end," he replied.

She felt his warm hand, for the first time, touch her panties and she shivered. She tried to concentrate and noticed, at last, that two of the numbers were out of alignment with the others in the columns. That was it?

"Sir, that's barely a mis—"

Whack! Whack! She jumped and squealed with the suddenness of it.

"Sir!"

More blows rained down, this time on her other cheek. Emily began moving her ass around to cool it off.

"Because there are two numbers out of alignment," he said smoothly, "that's twelve swats."

Twelve! That was more than she had ever endured before! How could she sit afterward? She'd be ruined, or discovered! He couldn't do this!

"Sir!"

Whack! Whack!

"That's six. Just six more."

"Ohhhh." Emily felt as if her body was on fire. Wiggling her bottom only caused her clit to bump against the desk and she was mortified at having another climax in front of him. How could she endure twelve strokes?

He struck her twice more. Emily pushed her ass back to give plenty of clearance so she wouldn't accidentally bump the desk. She bit her lip and hung on, tears now clouding her vision.

Whack! Whack!

"Just two more."

She nodded and braced herself. Her pussy seemed alive with sensations. Why did it like it so much? It wasn't right, it wasn't right, it wasn't right...

Whack! Whack!

Emily shuddered and tried to deny her body's release. *Don't bump the desk!* she screamed in her head. Just a few more seconds and she'd be okay. Then she could retreat to the restroom to relieve her powerful itch. *Just hold on!*

Suddenly, she felt Mr. Caudry's hands on her hips, pressing her forward, and she tried to fight it. Then one of his hands snaked around her hips and his fingers pressed hard against her clit and she was lost.

"Ohhhhhhh!" She groaned, a climax exploding through her. "Oh my god!" Her body shook and her vision blurred down to nothing for a few seconds as the sensations cascaded through her. She slumped down onto the desk, her legs too weak to support her.

She heard the clink of glasses and Mr. Caudry brought her another small brandy. She lifted herself up to sip it, grateful for a few more seconds before she had to face him. When she looked into his eyes, she could see an understanding.

"It's all right. I made you do it," he said.

She shook her head. "It was so wrong, so wrong."

"But you needed it so badly. You were hovering there. I didn't want you to waste it in the ladies restroom."

Emily's eyes opened in shock. "How did you..."

"Don't worry—I don't have any spies or cameras in there. I could just tell. The way you looked when you returned. It was obvious."

She blushed anew and looked away. "Mr. Caudry, this violates so many workplace rules!"

He laughed and the sound startled her. She had never heard him laugh before. She glanced up and saw a full smile. It made her heart give a sudden leap.

"Oh, Miss Robinson, I think we've gone beyond workplace rules, don't you?"

She wasn't sure how she felt about it. It was wrong, yes, but it also made her feel so good. Her mother would've said, "Anything that feels that good is probably bad for you." Maybe she was right.

"But I can't be doing this! I could get into trouble." She realized as soon as she said it how it could be taken the wrong way. "Trouble" could mean getting pregnant, which would tell him she was thinking someday they'd be having sex. But that wasn't what she had meant. She worried that by giving in to this dark side, she might lose complete control of her own body. Mr. Caudry would become her master, her universe.

As if to underscore those fears, he said, "Not to worry. You just leave that to me."

She found herself nodding. It was so easy to go along with this powerful man. His voice mesmerized her. And his touch! His touch sent her to the moon and back.

She rose and straightened out her skirt. "I'd better fix those mistakes," she said and picked up the report.

"Don't bother," he said and she realized he had been looking for any excuse to punish her. And at that moment, she knew she had lost more control over her life. Even if she never made another mistake, Mr. Caudry would somehow find some reason to bring her in to spank her. And now that he'd broken down the barrier of touching her, what could be next? She shivered.

"Yes, sir." She left, feeling hollow inside.

That evening, as Emily drank her wine and paced in the kitchen, she argued with herself. Quit, don't quit. Quit and get away from his control and demands. Don't quit because you need the money—and you really do like what he does to you. That was the confusing part, admitting to her desires. Face it, she was falling for this man! Was it because he reminded her of her father? She decided she was just too isolated and wondered if Julie could help her. But to admit all this to Julie—how embarrassing would that be? Would she make her show her sore bottom? Her best friend might laugh at her—or worse, tell her to quit on the spot.

That last part made Emily stand up straight. She didn't want to have someone tell her to quit because she didn't want to. As much as her mind told her to get out, her body said, "Let's see where this goes. Just for a little while longer."

***

She was out of sexy panties the next morning and realized she had forgotten to buy new ones. So she put on the new French cut ones with the lacy edges. Surely those would be all right. She wore a tan skirt that came to her knees and a light blue blouse. In the mirror, she looked quite the professional.

At work, she waited nervously for Mr. Caudry. Yesterday, he had made her show him her panties right away—would he do that again? Would it become a regular part of their morning? It was so wrong and yet her pussy throbbed with need.

When he came in, she found herself standing to greet him, as if he was a visiting dignitary. "Hello, Mr. Caudry."

He nodded and jerked his head toward his office. Quietly, she followed him inside.

"Show me," he said and she bit her lip.

"Mr. Caudry—" she began and he cut her off with a wave of her hand.

"That's one."

One? One what? Then she knew. One mistake. Now he was making her pay for mistakes in behavior! She lifted her skirt to show him her new yellow panties. He stared at her crotch for a long time and she felt like a little girl who had just spilled her juice.

"I thought we discussed what was acceptable," he said at last.

"But sir, I didn't have any clean—"

"A useless excuse. That's two."

Her face blushed red. Her mouth opened and closed but no sound came out. She wanted to drop her skirt and flee but she could only stand there, waiting for some guidance from her boss. How sick was that?

"We're up to seven per mistake, so that means fourteen swats," he said casually. She knew she could never stand that. Could she? Or would she collapse into a puddle of orgasms, making her humiliation worse?

"But I'll give you a choice," he continued and her spirits lifted. A choice! Anything was better than fourteen strokes with that dammed ruler! "I want you to remove those panties and place them on my desk. If you do, I'll cut your punishment in half."

She stared at him, her body trembling. She couldn't explain why she found herself dropping the skirt and reaching underneath to slide her panties down her thighs. He held up a hand and she froze.

"Tuck your skirt in first, in front."

Emily stared at him, afraid to move. He would see everything—he might even see how wet she was right now! That couldn't happen! "Uh, sir—"

"Are you arguing with me? Then forget it. That's three. Assume the position or get out."

"Please, sir," she said as she tucked her skirt up and stripped her panties down. "Please don't do that! See? I'm doing it."

He paused. "Stand up straight."

She did and watched as he stared at her now naked pussy, covered only by her tuft of pubic hair. Her arousal was obvious, she was certain. She wanted to melt into the floor. After a long time, he nodded. "Very well. For obeying me despite your embarrassment, I'll go easy and make it ten strokes."

Emily started to get into position when she realized he was about to spank her on her bare bottom! She wanted to protest, to run from the office, but she dared not risk his ire. Meekly, she leaned over the desk. Her skirt was still tucked in at the front, and when he tucked in the back part, she was completely exposed.

He retrieved the ruler and turned on the radio. He leaned down next to her and said, "You were pretty loud last time, so I'm going to gag you."

Her eyes went wide. *Gag me!*

"Don't worry, it's for your own protection. I'm sure you don't want those cubicle drones to hear your punishments, now do you?"

She shook her head and felt a silk handkerchief being slipped into place in her mouth. He tied it tightly in the back of her head. She had a sudden vision of herself: Hunched over his desk, naked ass and pussy on display, a gag in her mouth. She must look like a real slut.

Whack! Whack!

The ruler felt sharp against her bare skin, much worse than before. She gasped and moaned into the gag. Her bottom began its dance of avoidance.

Two more blows and already her orgasm was building within her. She was helpless to stop it, even if she wanted to. She knew he would force it from her if she didn't allow it to erupt spontaneously. She allowed her clit to bump against the edge of the desk.

Whack! Whack!

Her bottom was on fire now. How could she stand four more? She'd never make it. She moaned and danced and pleaded with him into her gag. She tried to keep her hips from the desk, but they seemed to have a mind of their own.

Twice more Emily was struck and she could barely stand now, her body was shaking and her feet were dancing up and down as she tried to wiggle away from his blows. Her orgasm was like a tsunami, roaring at her and she felt helpless before it. One more bump and she'd be lost.

Whack! Whack!

Her hips jutted forward, mashing her clit against the desk and she humped it, not caring that Mr. Caudry was watching her. Her orgasm washed over her and she collapsed onto the desk. She shook and mewed into her gagged, waves of pleasure rolling through her like ripples on a pond. This went against everything she had been taught. Sex was meant to be shared with someone you love—sex wasn't meant to be experienced in your boss's office, spread out over his desk, your ass up and willing.

Unless she was already in love with this man.

As she started to come down from her high, she felt Mr. Caudry's body press up against her and could not muster an objection as his hand once again came around to her bare clit. She felt his fingers expertly dip into her wetness to draw up the moisture to her clit and rub her hard. She came again in seconds, her body shaking once again and she knew she was lost now. She was at his mercy. No one had ever made her feel this way.

He stepped back and silence fell in the room, except for the radio playing jazz. From that moment on, Emily would associate jazz music with sex and would find herself lubricating at once, just like Pavlov's dogs.

As before, Mr. Caudry seemed dismissive, but his voice was soft. "You may go." He untied her gag and slipped it from her mouth.

She gathered herself up and pressed her skirt down with her hands. Her pussy still trembled underneath. She glanced at Caudry's desk, seeing the spot of yellow there and wondered if she should ask for them back. Her eyes raised to his and he gave a tiny shake of his head. She imagined him touching them, holding them to his nose and she left, that image burning into her mind. She paused and stared out over the cubicle farm to see one or two of the nearest workers glancing up at her. Did they know? Could they hear? She went at once to the ladies room to clean up.

Later, Emily sat at her desk feeling very strange without her panties. She worried that somehow, people might suspect. She kept her legs together and tried not to rise from her computer unless she had to.

Twice that day, Mr. Caudry asked her into his office, but not for punishments. Once he wanted coffee and another time to clarify a report detail. Each time, Emily could see her panties lying on his desktop, reminding her of her nakedness.

CHAPTER SEVEN

All that had occurred on Tuesday. She had been at her new job exactly seven days and she had somehow allowed herself to be manipulated into being a little whore for her boss. She had no doubt that her torment would continue. He would demand more and she would give in. Why? Because she like the orgasms?

There was more to it that than, wasn't there? Did she see a future with this man? Was she really in love with him? If so, how could that be? Hadn't she learned her lesson from her experience with Adam?

Despite her reservations, she now felt she needed to talk to Julie. She could give a perspective on the matter. Emily wouldn't tell her everything, just enough to get a reaction from her friend. She called her at once and told her she had "a situation" at work and could she come over?

Julie was there within twenty minutes, her face eager.

"What? What's happening? You look flushed. Are you all right?"

"Yes, I'm fine. Here, I've poured us some wine. I need it." Julie sat on the couch and Emily sat next to her, grimacing slightly from the pain she felt.

"Well, spill it, girl! You sounded so mysterious on the phone."

"Um. Okay. My boss at work, er, he's taking advantage of me."

Julie reared back, her face indignant. "No! Well, report him! Women don't have to put up with that kind of crap anymore."

"No, it's not like that." She suddenly felt acutely embarrassed and wondered if this was such a good idea.

"What's it like then? What's he doing?"

How could she say it? "Uh, well, let's just say what he's doing is turning me on. It shouldn't, but it is."

Julie's eyes went wide. "What? What's he doing? Come on, you can tell me!"

Emily looked down. She knew she had to say something. "He swats me. Playfully," she lied. "I know it's inappropriate and all, but I kinda like it."

Julie took a big sip and put her glass down. She leaned forward and tipped up Emily's face so she could see into her eyes. "You like it? You mean that?"

She nodded, feeling her eyes fill up with tears. "I know it's wrong and all. But I find it strangely sexy. I'm not sure what to do about it."

"Wow." Julie was silent for a while as she soaked it all in. "That's all? Just swats you? In what way, 'Atta girl' or 'You need to be punished, you bad girl'?"

Emily stared at her shoes and Julie had her answer. "Punishment? You get off on that?"

"Don't make me sound like a freak! I'm so embarrassed, I didn't know who else to turn to!"

"Hey, it's okay. You can always talk to me."

Emily nodded. "I was hoping you could explain it all to me so I know what to do. In some ways it reminds me of Adam and that scares me." Julie had heard all about Emily's disastrous relationship with her almost fiancé.

"Well, let me ask you some questions." She ticked them off on her fingers. "One, do you like this guy? I mean, could you see yourself having a relationship with him if he wasn't your boss?"

Good question, Emily thought. Hard to answer. "I don't know. At first, I hated him because he was so mean. Kind of a sourpuss, you know. But after this started, I started looking at him differently. I don't know if I could ever consider him a boyfriend, though. He's much older than I am."

"How much older?"

"I don't know for sure, but I'd say he's around forty."

"That's not old! That's only nine-ten years. Eleven at the most." She shook her head. "Okay, two: How did this start? What prompted it?"

"Uh, I made some mistakes and he said he'd have to let me go. I begged him for another chance and he said he'd spank me instead. So that's how it started."

"And now he spanks you for every mistake, right?"

Emily nodded. "Right."

"Through your skirt?"

"Yeah," she lied, too embarrassed to admit how far she had gone.

"He uses his hand?"

"Mostly. Sometimes a ruler." God, she was lying through her teeth.

"So it doesn't really hurt then?"

"No, not really. But it makes me feel really funny inside. You know."

"What do you do about that feeling?"

"Uh. God, I'm so embarrassed!"

"Come on, Em! You called me. I'm trying to help."

"Well, often I have to go into the rest room and, uh, you know..."

Julie's faced registered her surprise. "Right there at work? Wow, you got it bad, girl."

"You're not making me feel any better!"

"Okay," she laughed and then suppressed it. "Sorry. All right. Three: Do you feel you should report him?"

"Well, that's the thing. I'm a lowly secretary and he's a top salesman, so if someone were to be let go, it would be me."

"That's no excuse for that kind of behavior! You could sue!"

Emily held up her hand. "No, I can't blame him alone. It's also...Well, like I said, I get really turned on. More so than I ever have before. I'm torn, you see. It feels good and yet..."

"You never felt this way with Adam, did you? I mean, back when it was good?"

Emily bit her lip. "Uh, no."

"Yeah. Okay. Let's review. So you kinda like this guy but he acts like a boss, not a boyfriend, right?"

Emily nodded.

"And you find yourself really turned on by his actions, even though you know they're wrong."

"Yes. So what should I do?"

Julie smiled. "Girl, you gotta marry this guy."

"What!?"

"Come on! No employee in her right mind would put up with that unless she really, really liked it. Which you admit that you do. Face it, girl, you like a strong man like your boss."

Emily already knew that, but it sounded good coming from Julie. "You think? What does that make me, some kind of doormat?"

"Hell no. You're submissive. Oh, don't look so shocked. Some women just are. Nothing wrong with it."

Is that what I am? she thought. *A submissive?* "What about you?"

"Me? Nah. I like to be in charge. Which might explain why I'm still single!"

"So it's a bad thing or not? I'm confused."

"No, it's not a bad thing. You just get off on letting a guy, um, control you. Or whatever. You find it incredibly sexy."

"But that's the thing—Adam wanted to control me and that was a disaster!"

"Oh, honey, this guy's got it all over Adam. He was nothing but an abuser. Your Mr. Caudry sounds like a true dom."

"Dom?"

"Dominant. Jeez, girl, don't you ever look online?"

"No, I guess I don't. Maybe I should, huh?"

"Yeah," Julie said. "So you know what's going on."

"Does this mean Mr. Caudry won't turn out like Adam?"

"No, it usually doesn't. I mean, sure, some Doms go too far. But mostly, they pay careful attention to their subs, so they can give them what they want. And girl, you admitted he's already doing that."

"Yeah, I guess so." She paused. "What do you mean, too far?"

"Oh, I don't know. Depends on the guy. But it could mean whips and chains, body piercings, tattoos, dungeons..."

Emily looked horrified. "No!" She couldn't imagine Mr. Caudry doing anything like that. He always seemed to be in complete control. And yet, how far might he go if she didn't stop him?

Julie shrugged. "I'm just saying. That's worst case scenario. Then again, you might like it." She winked.

"I'm not that bad!"

"You never know until you try. The key thing here is trust. I mean, if you're both into it, fine. But if he's into it and you're not and you find yourself going along with it despite your better judgment, then it can become a problem."

"So I should find out just how far this might go before I get in over my head."

"Exactly. You don't want to wake up one day to find yourself gagged and tied to a cross while a guy whips you and you can't stop him."

Emily felt two sensations at once. Dread from being so helpless and vulnerable and that damned throbbing in her pussy that told her she wanted it, needed it.

"Thanks. You've, uh, helped."

"Really?"

"Yeah."

They both sipped their wine and thought their private thoughts.

CHAPTER EIGHT

Wednesday morning, Emily realized with a sudden horror she had still failed to buy new underwear. Cursing, she rinsed out her new blue ones, the only ones Mr. Caudry had liked, and tossed them in the dryer for a few minutes. When she got out of the shower, they were still damp, but she had run out of time. She put them on, grimacing at the coolness and hurried to work.

When he showed up, she was already rising, ready to do her duty. She followed him inside and found herself lifting her skirt before he even asked her to. He studied her panties and nodded. She started to lower her skirt.

"Wait."

She stopped at once, her skirt still up. He came forward and she wanted to say something, anything to drown out the roaring in her ears.

"Sir..." she whispered.

"Shhh," he said. His hand touched the front of her panties and she knew he could feel the dampness. "They're wet."

"I had to rinse them. There was nothing else clean." Her voice was barely audible.

"Damp panties are unacceptable."

In that moment, Emily realized he wasn't talking about simply dampness from the wash. He was now controlling her very arousal. And he would find her aroused often—she couldn't help it. More excuses for spankings, she thought.

"You know what to do."

"Please, sir..."

"That's two."

She moved into position, her body trembling. She watched him retrieve the ruler and heard the radio go on. Immediately, her pussy grew wet and swollen. Emily felt him tuck her skirt under her waist. She waited for her punishment like an obedient subject. But when she felt his fingers tugging at the sides of her panties, she rebelled.

"Sir! What are you doing?"

"That's three. You know that as you continue to disobey, the punishments increase. From now on, you must be punished on your bare bottom."

"Ohhhh," she moaned, feeling her panties being removed from her. He made her lift her legs one at a time so he could free them and she obeyed meekly. He placed them on the desk in front of her, so she could see her humiliation.

"Since we're up to eight, and you made three mistakes, that's twenty-four swats with the ruler," he informed her.

Twenty-four! She could never endure that. "Please, sir..."

"That's four."

She groaned. Now it was thirty-two? She began to cry.

"There, there," he said softly, one hand on her ass, stroking her. "I'm willing to make another deal with you to reduce your punishment."

"Yes, sir?" There was some hope after all. But at what price?

He reached around her and tugged gently on her pubic hair. "You can have thirty-two swats on your bottom, or ten swats on your pussy."

Emily thought her knees would give out completely. She sagged against the desktop, her mind in complete turmoil. Her pussy!? He wanted to spank her pussy? That's...that's awful. So very, very wrong.

But compared to thirty-two swats, what choice did she have? It never occurred to her to call the whole thing off, to quit or to report him. She could no longer think in those terms.

"M-my p-pussy, sir."

"Very well. Get up on the desk on your back."

Now he would see everything. Her body's most intimate part would be exposed. She wished he had asked to see her breasts instead! But her pussy! It represented the very core of her. Groaning, she climbed up on the desk and rolled over. She kept her legs together as long as she dared before allowing him to open her up, pressing her knees down on the desk to either side. She felt like she was being butterflied.

"You must hold your legs in position."

Tears clouded her eyes as she obeyed. She could only imagine what he saw—a pretty young woman, naked from the waist down, sobbing quietly as she was completely exposed.

He wasted no time.

Whack!

The ruler was wielded carefully, not nearly as hard as when she was spanked on her ass, but it still stung. She jerked and started to snap her legs together before her mind overruled her body and she remained in place.

He struck her again and the pain flashed briefly, followed by heat spreading throughout her loins, making her aware that she could easily climax from this punishment. How could that be? How could a woman react to such torture by experiencing pleasure?

Whack!

She groaned and Mr. Caudry paused. She was grateful for the break. But he only stopped long enough to tie the silk scarf around her head as a gag. She could taste the material and hoped it could keep her quiet.

When he struck her again, she knew the orgasm was coming now and there was nothing she could do to stop it. She could only hope she could hang on long enough so he would be finished first.

Whack!

"That's five," he told her and she shook her head from side to side. Only five! She despaired.

When he slapped the ruler down again, her legs snapped together as a thunderous orgasm rocked her. She keened into her gag and lay on her side as the sensations short-circuited her brain. It felt like it went on forever. Finally she came back to her senses and looked up to see Mr. Caudry standing there, holding the ruler, smiling down at her.

"Only four more to go," he said.

She shook her head, pleading with him, but it did no good. She was made to lie back and spread open once more.

Whack!

The blows were softer now, she noticed at once. He was being gentle and it pleased her.

Whack!

She shuddered and felt another orgasm out there. Could it be?

Whack!

Her hips shook and she could feel it growing within her.

Whack!

The final blow brought her right to the brink—so close! Without thinking, she reached her hand down and rubbed herself to a shuddering climax. She no longer cared that her boss was watching her, she had to come!

When she came down from her high, a wave of embarrassment washed over her when she realized what she had done.

"I'm sorry," she squeaked.

"Don't be. That's going to be a new rule."

"What?"

"From now on, you are not allowed to climax in the bathroom. And don't think you can sneak around, because it's obvious to me when you have come."

"But...but...where..."

"You'll come in here and have an orgasm in front of me."

Emily shook her head. She was getting in deeper and deeper. Julie had been right—Mr. Caudry knew no limits—at least as far as she could see.

He frowned at her resistance. "Or," he said, leaning down close and giving her damp pussy a kiss. "You can let me do it. Either way, the only time you can come is in front of me."

Watching her boss kiss her pussy woke her up and she rolled off the desk, snatched up her panties and yanked them into place. With a wild look at Mr. Caudry, she fled. He said nothing to stop her.

She paused outside, not sure what to do. She spotted a few curious looks among the other workers and tried to pretend everything was all right. But it was far from all right. He was moving too fast and she didn't know how to stop him. She gathered up her purse and left, not sure what she should do.

Emily drove straight home and locked her door. She sat on the couch and tried not to think about what had just happened. He had kissed her pussy!

Let me get this straight, that naughty voice said to her sarcastically. *You thought it was okay to get ten swats on your bare pussy and come twice, but when he kissed your pussy afterwards, you freaked out?*

Well, yeah, she responded to herself. It did sound silly, the way her inner voice put it. But still, none of it was right. *I don't care if I climaxed. It's just not right!*

You have a lot to learn, the voice said.

The phone rang. She jumped and debated answering it. Finally she gave in and picked it up.

"Hello?"

"Miss Robinson? Are you feeling ill?" Her boss's voice chilled her.

"Uh, yeah. I am."

"Will you be in tomorrow?"

His tone seemed...different. More concerned. Not at all like the domineering boss she had grown used to.

"Yes," she said, deciding right then and there that she needed to return. She wasn't about to lose her job now!

"Very well. I hope you feel better." He rang off.

It was as simple as that. Perhaps Mr. Caudry had realized he had pushed her too far.

Emily got up and stripped off her work clothes and put on some jeans and a tee-shirt. She decided to go out and shop as a way of distracting herself. Anything to get the image out of her mind. Even now, whenever she closed her eyes, she could see herself, spread out and waiting for Mr. Caudry's ruler. She shuddered.

She drove to the mall and shopped, not really expecting to buy much. Payday was still two days away. But when she found herself among the bras and panties she remembered she needed some new ones. She selected several pairs she liked and whittled them down to three. That was all she could afford for the moment. Looking over her selections, she realized she had unconsciously chosen panties Mr. Caudry would approve of. There was one pair of bikinis in pale purple, and two pairs of thongs, one ivory and one red. She stared at them, wondering if she should put them back. Shaking her head, she knew not to have them would only cause more punishments. She went to the cashier and bought them all.

Back home, she sat on the couch and drank an entire bottle of wine as she tried to sort out her feelings. She had gone so far now—how much further was she willing to go? When she had left, she had almost made up her mind to quit, yet she found herself listening more to that dark part of her that told her she needed it. Julie had even said she was a submissive.

Is this what I'm supposed to do? Let my feelings control me? Or should I be listening to my head instead?

The answer was obvious. Her brain loved the orgasms as much as her pussy did. Even now, despite her fears, she wanted to see where it went. If it got too scary, she could bail out at any time. She was like a trapeze artist, working above a net. If she ever fell, she could walk away unharmed.

Right?

The next day, Thursday, she showered and dressed and paused in front of her dresser, looking over the three new pairs of underwear she had bought. By all rights, she should wear the bikinis—they would give her some coverage and Mr. Caudry would accept them. For some reason, she chose the red thong instead. She couldn't explain why. Trying not to think, she slipped them on and found a white lace bra. She chose a red skirt to match her panties and a white satin top that really didn't show much. She looked...safe, she decided. Only she and Mr. Caudry would know what she had on underneath.

She waited nervously at work for her boss to show up. He came in and nodded and she followed him into his office. Once the door was closed, she lifted up her skirt to show him her thong. He whistled.

"That's great," he said. "I'm glad to see you still want to work here. I was worried, after yesterday."

"You scared me, that's all."

"I apologize."

Her heart fluttered. He was apologizing! To her!

He stepped forward and she braced herself. His hand touched the front of the tiny panel that covered her pussy and tsked.

"What?"

"I like the panties, but this hair will have to go." He tugged at some of her downy fleece that spilled out around it.

Every tug felt as if he was rubbing her clit. She sucked in her breath and wished he would stop. But she didn't ask him to. Nor did she question his order. She merely stood there and tried not to come as his fingers teased her.

"Hmmm. You can shave it or I can send you to a salon I know and they'll give you a wax."

Emily closed her eyes. The choice she was being offered was an illusion. "Which would you like, Mr. Caudry?"

She could hear the smile in his voice. "Oh, the wax. Much more permanent. And it doesn't leave that awful stubble. I'll set it up for your lunch period."

She nodded and stood there, skirt up, waiting for his command.

He stepped back. "You may go."

Emily dropped her skirt and went at once to her desk. Without thinking about lunch, she got to work. He called her in after a while and asked her to bring him some coffee. She nodded and went at once to the break room. She spotted Mrs. Dowd and skidded to a halt.

"How are things going with Mr. Caudry?" the woman asked, stirring something into her coffee.

"Oh, fine. We had a little bit of a rough start, but I'm starting to learn what he likes."

"Oh, good," she said, smiling. "I was hoping you'd work out. So many girls came and went in that position. I despaired ever finding someone who would put up with him."

"He's...he's not so bad when you get to know him," she found herself answering and felt a twinge of embarrassment when Mrs. Dowd looked up sharply at her. Then her face softened.

"Well, that's nice. You let me know if you have any problems." She tottered away.

Emily, her gaze following her, thought: *You mean, like if Mr. Caudry demands I show him my panties every day and spanks me if I make a mistake? Like that?*

She made his coffee and returned to set it on his desk.

"Thank you," he said and she basked in the simple pleasantry.

She didn't make any mistakes that morning and when lunchtime came around, Emily had almost forgotten about her "appointment." Mr. Caudry reminded her. He handed her a business card and said, "Go here and ask for Arlene. She's expecting you. Everything's paid for."

She took the card and read it: Arlene's Beauty Emporium. It had an address on Lancaster, just a few blocks away. She looked up. "Are you sure?"

He frowned. "Of course I'm sure." He left her standing there, holding the card.

Resigned, she headed out to find the shop. Her nerves grew as she neared it and she nearly backed out. But she knew Mr. Caudry would be so disappointed. She couldn't face that. So she went in and asked for Arlene.

A bleached blonde of about fifty came forward. "Oh, you must be Emily. Come on back." She led her through a door into a small room where a padded chair, somewhat like a barber's chair, was bolted to the floor. Emily felt fear shoot through her.

"Um..."

"Don't worry, I've been doing this for years. Guaranteed results. All the girls are doing it nowadays."

"Will it hurt?"

"Just a little. Like a pinch." She handed her a smock. "Here, take off your clothes and put this on, opening to the front and get into the chair."

Arlene left without another word and Emily quietly stripped and stacked her clothes on the counter. She pulled on the gown and tried to tie the two straps in front but only the top one was whole. The bottom tie had both sides ripped off. She held the sides together as she climbed into the barber's chair.

Arlene came in at once and stepped on a lever, causing the chair to tip back suddenly. Emily hung on, afraid she might get thrown out.

"Oh, sorry, that pedal sticks. I need to oil it. Now hang on while I adjust these straps." She began tying Emily's thighs, stomach and arms down against the chair.

"Wait, what—"

Arlene ignored her and quickly completed her task, leaving her helpless. Emily quickly learned that Arlene one of those breezy blondes who liked to talk. She began chatting up a storm as she began turning a crank, which caused Emily's legs to be pulled apart. She tried to protest, but she could hardly get a word in edgewise. Arlene yanked the smock apart, exposing her pussy to her gaze.

"This isn't too bad. You never shaved it or anything? Well, that's a surprise. You should see all the cuties that come in here and ask that it all be yanked out. They say a boy won't go down on them unless they do. Ha! Isn't that a hoot! Why, my Milton wouldn't go down on me unless I turned twenty again, hair or no hair!" She guffawed at her own joke.

"Will it ever grow back?" She feared being denuded for the rest of her life.

"Oh, sure, but not for months, maybe longer. You'll need to come in for another session in about six months, but then it might last a whole year. Now you, having light brown hair, shouldn't have too much trouble. You should see some of the darker complexioned gals who come in! Whooeee, do they have hair! And it grows fast. I had one gal in here, I swear, she was growing kudzu!"

And on she went while Emily lay there, terrified. Why was she doing this? Each time she vowed to give her job another try, she found herself being drawn in deeper. She really must ask him to slow down! It was all going way too fast!

Arlene smeared some warm wax from a tub over the edge of her hairy triangle and pressed a strip of cloth into it. "Now, I've found the best way to handle this is to think about something else," she said and reached up and pinched one of Emily's nipples, hard.

"Ow!"

At the same time, with her other hand, Arlene yanked the strip free.

"OOOOW!"

"See? How'd that work?"

"That was terrible! Stop it! It hurts!"

"Don't be a baby. Now if you don't like that, there is another way."

"What? I've changed my mind. Let me up!"

"Ohh, Mr. Caudry would be mad about that, don't you think? Here, let me distract you." With that, she reached in and began to rub her pussy expertly, making her wet.

"Stop that," she gasped and tried to wiggle away. There was nowhere to go.

"Oh, hush. You'll thank me later." She paused long enough to spread some more wax on the other side and press down another strip of cloth, then her fingers returned to drive her to the brink.

"Oh! Oh!"

Arlene yanked away the strip and Emily would've shot straight out of her chair except for the straps holding her in place.

"There, doesn't that look better already?"

Emily looked down to see her fuzzy triangle had become a landing strip. "That's enough, please, it hurts!"

The hairdresser's hand returned to her pussy and teased her. Emily forgot her protests and began shaking her hips, ready to come at any moment. Once again, Arlene pulled away to smear some more wax over her remaining hair.

"Please," Emily begged.

"Don't worry, just a sec. Keep your fires burning." She pressed one more strip over the wax and pleasured Emily for a few minutes until it was obvious the girl was about to come. Then she yanked the strip off at the same time she rubbed the girl's clit hard.

"YEEEOOOOWW!" Emily was caught between her orgasm and her pain as she thrashed in the chair. The orgasm finally won and she went with it, glad to have the pleasure overcome everything else.

Arlene used a few smaller strips to remove the remaining hair before declaring, "There, you're all done."

You're right about that, she thought. She looked down to see her reddened pussy was completely bare. It made her look like a girl again. Arlene unstrapped her and helped her up. Emily was almost too weak to stand.

"Okay, you're all set. Come back in six months for a touch-up." She left to allow Emily to don her clothes in peace. She gingerly touched her mound and marveled at how it felt, so soft and smooth. She felt her pussy tingle again and jerked her hand away.

What was happening to her? She was becoming so easily aroused all the time now.

When she returned from lunch, Mr. Caudry buzzed and asked her to come into his office. She knew what he wanted. Sighing to herself, she went in and stood before his desk. He simply nodded and she lifted her skirt as if it wasn't a strange demand at all.

"Wait, I can't see," he said. "Take down your thong."

Emily opened her mouth to protest but the words died in her throat. After having Arlene work her over, was it really any big deal to show the results to the man who had paid for it? She lowered the front of her thong with one hand while keeping her skirt raised with the other.

"Ohhh, that's nice," he said, coming around his desk to step close.

Emily felt the heat rise in her body and she fought to stand still.

"I want to touch it to feel how smooth it is."

It wasn't really a question, it was more of a command. She closed her eyes and simply nodded. She felt the pads of his fingers on her bare mound, moving around gently. It was still sore and she winced.

"Sorry. I'm trying to be gentle."

She nodded and said nothing. He *was* being gentle. Too gentle—she felt her arousal quicken and her breath caught in her throat. His fingers moved down to part the folds of skin where her wetness had gathered. Her mouth came open. His hand went to her thong and eased it from her fingers. She felt it slip down her legs and puddle around her ankles.

"Step out of them. Move your legs apart."

Emily obeyed, not sure why she should be allowing this. But it felt so good. His fingers slid the fluid up to her clit and he teased that marble of flesh. Emily began to sway on her feet and Mr. Caudry moved one arm around her waist to hold her steady.

"Does that feel good?"

"Yessss," she breathed, losing herself in the moment.

"How many orgasms have you had, since you started working here?"

The question caught her off guard and her climax retreated. "Uh, what?"

"Orgasms. How many have you had in the last two weeks?" His hand stilled and she found herself trying to hump his fingers. He pulled them away, just out of reach.

"I, uh, I don't know."

"Guess. Was it five, ten, fifteen?"

"Uh, maybe ten."

"Really? Counting all those ones in the bathroom? And at home after work?"

"Maybe fifteen."

"Do you think that's fair?"

"What? Fair? I, uh, don't..." She wasn't sure what he meant. She never wanted orgasms at work, not at first anyway. They just seemed to happen to her. His fingers returned to her clit and she groaned softly.

"Fair," he repeated, pulling away again. "Do you think it's fair?"

"I don't understand, sir."

"Do you think you're the only person who wants an orgasm?"

It hit her, then. Now the sex would start. She didn't want to, not so soon, and yet, her body craved release. And he was right—it was fair. She had come so far so fast, why not sex? Still, it was a lot to ask. Would this mean he was becoming her boyfriend?

"What do you want?"

"Same as what you're getting. That's all."

She felt a sense of relief. "Oh! Sure. I guess I can do that." A hand job in exchange for all the orgasms he's given her? It was so much less that she had expected.

He returned to his desk and sat down and she followed him, her pussy still weeping with need under her skirt. She tried to ignore it and knelt down beside his chair. She waited to be told what to do.

Mr. Caudry smiled. "Unzip me."

Emily nodded and unzipped his pants. She freed his cock and smiled. It was a very nice cock. She wrapped both hands around it and began to stroke. It swelled and she found her attention being drawn by that mysterious eye in the center, like a Cyclops staring at her. She rubbed his cock, up and down until her hands grew tired.

"You know what would help?" he said, startling her.

"What?"

"It would help if you'd unbutton your blouse. I've never seen your breasts."

Emily nodded. She was glad to release his cock and wiggle the feeling back into her fingers. She unbuttoned her blouse and opened it. She pushed her bra down below her breasts. He smiled and reached out and touched her, rubbing his fingers around her nipples. Each touch sent another shock down to her clit and she wanted nothing more than to come.

Rubbing her hands together to give her strength, she returned to his cock. She stroked him, up and down, up and down, for another ten minutes but it seemed as if she was doing it wrong. He just smiled down at her and watched.

Finally, her strength gave out and she felt tears come to her eyes. "I'm sorry, sir. My hands are just too tired."

"Well, that's unfortunate. You'd better return to work."

Disappointed in not being able to help him, but more saddened by her own unmet needs, Emily rose and straightened out her clothes. She found her thong and slipped it on. She headed for the door and Mr. Caudry stopped her before she could put her hand on the knob.

"I figure that's worth about twenty swats, don't you?"

She turned, her mouth agape. "What?"

"For failing to do your duty. You've gotten to come many times and yet I couldn't come once. Please return here at five for your punishment."

She knew the building emptied quickly and they would be alone. She started to say something, anything that would make him realize how unfair he was being. There was that word again. Fair. She could imagine, to him, she was being unfair to not allow him release. He was a man, after all. She found herself nodding and opened the door.

"Oh, and Miss Robinson?"

She turned.

"Don't sneak off to masturbate. If I can't come, you can't come."

Emily looked up quickly toward the cubicles, afraid his words might've carried. But other than a few glances, no one seemed to care what was happening in his office. She left quickly and closed the door gently behind her.

The afternoon dragged on. Her mound itched and she had to reach down often to scratch it, but she dared not go further. She had to pee and she worried that Mr. Caudry would assume she was masturbating, so she sat at her desk and squirmed.

Finally, just before five she couldn't take it anymore. She jumped up and ran to the bathroom and peed quickly. She washed her hands and made it back just in time to hear her intercom buzz.

"Yes, Mr. Caudry?"

"It's time."

She slipped inside and closed the door, ready for her punishment.

"Remove your clothes first."

She stopped halfway to his desk. "M-my clothes, sir?"

"Yes."

"But, sir!"

"That's twenty-five swats. Fifteen on your ass, ten on your pussy."

Her body was shaking as she stripped off her clothes. Everything was moving too fast, she thought. Was it less than two weeks ago that she had arrived here, full of hope and promise? And now look at her! Being ordered to strip naked in her boss's office and prepare herself to be spanked like a little girl.

And yet, she was doing it, just as he had demanded. What did that make her? She tossed her clothes onto a chair and stood before him naked, showing every part of her for the first time. She didn't have anything he hadn't seen, she told herself.

"Assume the position."

Emily hunched over the desk, her ass an inviting target. He removed the ruler and moved around behind her. She heard the radio go on and her pussy immediately flooded with fluids. She groaned before he even touched her.

"What was that?"

"Nothing, sir."

Whack! Whack! Her ass exploded in pain. He was not holding anything back this time. She bit her lip and tried not to scream. Was there anyone left in the office? Surely they could hear the sound they were making!

Whack! Whack!

"Please, sir! It hurts so much!"

"Then you'd better figure out a way to make me come. Otherwise, I'll have to take my frustrations out on your ass."

Whack! Whack!

"Let me try again! Please, sir!" Her ass danced and weaved as the pain flooded her senses.

He paused and she looked back at him, tears in her eyes, her expression hopeful.

"Very well. If you do a good job, I'll forgo the rest of the spankings to your bottom."

"Oh, thank you sir!" she babbled and followed him to his chair, her hands already unzipping him even as he sat down. She freed his cock and saw how her whipping had made him hard. She started in again with her hands, trying to coax his seed from him. But as she stroked, his dick seemed to soften slightly in her grip. Emily felt her panic rising. She couldn't face any more swats like those.

Without thinking about it, she plunged her mouth over his cock and began to suck. She was rewarded when she felt it swell again and she made love to that cock, teasing it with her tongue, playing it like a fine instrument. She kept one hand below to stroke the base, building his sensations, trying desperately to make him come.

"Yes," he whispered and she redoubled her efforts. Pushing the cock as far as she could down her throat and working at it with her tongue. She remembered every trick she had learned from her boyfriends.

Soon, she could hear him panting. Then a hoarse cry and suddenly, her mouth filled with his semen. Emily choked and coughed, pulling away so she could swallow some and spit out the rest into his waste basket.

Her happiness was short-lived. When she looked up, his expression was dark.

"What, sir?"

"You spit out my seed like it was vile? That will never do!"

"I'm sorry, sir! I was caught off guard!"

He nodded. "Very well. We'll call it first time jitters. I'm sure you'll do better next time."

Next time? she thought. Of course there will be a next time.

"Now get into position."

Emily stared at him, confused. "But sir! You said if I got you to come, you'd forgo the rest of my spanking!"

"I said I'd forgo the rest on your bottom. I still owe you ten on that beautiful bare pussy of yours."

She felt her breath catch in her throat and the world seemed to stop for a moment. Then her body began to move as if she had no control over it. She slowly climbed up onto the desk and lay on her back. He moved between her legs and pressed her knees down to the sides.

"You know the drill by now."

She nodded, trying not to cry.

The ruler struck her naked mound and she cried out, her body shaking. It was so much harsher now that she had no hair to cushion the blows!

Whack!

"Oh god, sir! It hurts!"

"As long as you obey the rules, you won't have to be punished at all," he said and she knew it was a lie. He liked it. He would always find a way to punish her.

With each blow, despite the pain, her orgasm rose up within her. She fought it, for certainly it made her look like a real slut. Who in their right mind would come when being slapped?

She couldn't help it, her legs closed and she shook with a small orgasm. "Ow! Ow! Oh god!" Pain and pleasure were all mixed up in her mind.

"That was disappointing," he said. "You only made it through four blows."

"Please, sir, my pussy is still sore from the waxing! Please! I can't take it!"

He relented. He seemed to be in a much better mood now that he had come. "Very well. I'll strike your tits for the last six. Three each."

She nodded, happy to sacrifice her breasts instead of her incredibly sore pussy. She scrambled up and sat on the edge of the desk.

"Present your breasts for punishment."

Emily lifted them up from underneath and grimaced as he prepared the ruler.

Whack! First the left one, right across the top. She winced and more tears flew from her eyes.

Now the right, leaving a red welt.

Back to the left, further down.

Same place on her right tit. She knew what was coming next and tried to brace herself.

Her left nipple exploded in pain and she squealed and shook.

Now the right nipple and she nearly fainted, jerking back out of the way and holding both hands over her breasts.

"Oh god, sir! Oh my god that hurts!"

"You may get dressed," was all he said. He was done with her.

She climbed back into her clothes, wincing every time her sore skin came in contact with them. He sat at his desk and watched.

When she was done, she stood there, waiting to be released.

"You may go. See you tomorrow."

She grabbed her purse from her desk and left without looking behind her.

CHAPTER TEN

Friday morning, Emily was standing in Mr. Caudry's office, her skirt held up as he examined her choice of panties. Today she was wearing the white thong. He seemed pleased.

"Excellent choice, my dear. Turn around."

She did, knowing how the thong disappeared into her crack of her ass, giving him a full view of her bottom. It still bore faint marks from the ruler.

"Great. You may lower your skirt."

She dropped it, relieved. It was short-lived.

"Now, I want a cup of coffee and a blowjob."

Emily looked up, shocked. Just like that? She couldn't move.

"What's wrong? Didn't you hear me?"

"Sir? You want a…" She couldn't say it.

"Yes, what man wouldn't? Remember, you're way ahead of me and I need to catch up. We discussed this, didn't we? Do I need to go over it again?"

She shook her head and left his office. Her hands trembled as she poured his coffee and added just the right amount of sugar. Two other workers were in the break room and she felt their eyes were on her, as if they knew what was happening to her. She wanted to scream, to cry out for help, but she said nothing. Something within her held her tongue still. Keeping her eyes down, she took the cup and brought it back to Mr. Caudry's office. She set it on his desk and waited.

He took a sip. "Ummm, good." He leaned back in his chair. "Well?"

Her legs took her around the desk without conscious thought. Then her knees buckled and she was face to face with his zipper. Emily felt tears come to her eyes and she looked up at him for some kind of reprieve. He leaned forward and put his hand alongside her jaw. She closed her eyes and rested her face in the palm of his hand. For a moment, she thought he might relent.

"If you'd prefer, I can punish you instead."

Her eyes flew open. "N-no, sir," she said and her hands went to his zipper. His cock was already hard and she took it into her mouth before she could think about what she was doing. Once she tasted it, her mouth took over and she licked and sucked him until she could tell he was about to come. She pulled back at the last moment and tasted his seed as he squirted. This time, she swallowed almost all of it, allowing just a few drops to leak around the edges of her lips.

"Ohhhh!" he groaned, holding her head. "That was wonderful!"

Emily couldn't breathe but she didn't complain or try to pull away. She waited until he released her before she pulled off of his cock and sucked in air.

"You did very well, just a few drops leaked out, I see. I'm very pleased."

She nodded and wiped her mouth. Her pussy ached and she wanted nothing more than to have him rub her until she came.

He seemed to know what she was thinking. "How about you, Emily? Would you like to come too?"

It was the first time he had called her Emily. She nodded as gratitude washed over her.

"Well, that would be a problem, wouldn't it? I mean, if you come every time I come, I'd never catch up, would I?" He sat there, his cock peeking from his pants, his head tipped to one side.

That confused her. What did it matter? Didn't he like it when she came?

"But I'm willing to work with you."

She nodded, eager for him to find a solution.

"I'll spank you while you masturbate. When you come, I'll stop."

Emily's mouth dropped open. How could she do that? It would be too embarrassing! She might never come—and then he might never stop spanking her! "Uh, sir..."

"Let's try it, shall we?"

By his tone, she knew there could be no argument. She nodded and rose to her feet. He stopped her.

"No, not over the desk this time. We're going to do it a bit differently. We'll do it right here, next to my desk. I want you to remove your thong and get down on your knees."

While she obeyed, he went to the radio and turned it on. Her pussy wept. He returned and rummaged in his desk drawer. When he pulled out a short section of rope, Emily felt a thrum of panic roil through her. Mr. Caudry ordered her to hold her hands out and she obeyed.

"Mr. Caudry—" she began when she saw he was tying her hands in front of her.

"You must learn to obey the rules," he responded. When he was done, she wiggled her fingers and found the rope wasn't too tight and she nodded.

He told her to bend all the way over until her face was on the rug. Without the use of her hands, she found it made her feel even more vulnerable. He made her wiggle her knees up tight until her ass was pointed up in the air. The skirt fell down around her waist. Even that wasn't enough.

"Now move your knees apart so I can see the pretty pussy of yours."

She did, feeling exposed and foolish. His hand touched her ass and suddenly, all she could think about was her wet pussy, just inches away from his fingers. She wiggled her bottom at him.

"Now do you think you can be quiet?"

She nodded, which was difficult with her cheek pressed against the rug.

"Very well." She heard the drawer open and waited, her body a bundle of nerves.

"Put your hands between your legs. That's is, right there on your pussy. Oh, it's so wet, isn't it? Now as soon as I begin, you may begin. When I see evidence of your climax, I'll stop."

"Oh, god," she whispered.

"What was that?"

"Nothing, sir."

"Very well." There came a moment of silence, followed by the sharp crack of the ruler. She jerked and immediately her fingers began rubbing herself hard as she desperately wanted to come.

Her fingers rubbed and rubbed but she was distracted by that damned ruler!

He alternated, left and right, never giving her a rest. Her fingers were a blur but her orgasm hung just out of reach. Yet it seemed to build on itself, growing larger and larger within her.

With each blow, her mind stopped distinguished between pleasure and pain. Her pussy was gaping, runny with fluids and she knew he was looking right at it as she debased herself. And suddenly something broke inside her and she realized she *wanted* him to look at her, she wanted to be used and abused and to obey his commands.

Her hand went to her pussy and began to rub in earnest now and felt her orgasm rush at her.

She discovered the spanking was actually helping now and she rose quickly toward her release. Her body shuddered and she cried out, her climax rocked her just as the final blow from the ruler hit her sore bottom.

She felt transported. She didn't know exactly what had happened to her or why, only that her mind seemed to leave her body for a few seconds. She gasped when she realized how powerfully her climax had hit her. It was like nothing she had ever experienced before. It took several moments for her mind to come back to earth.

He untied her hands and helped her up. She was shaky and needed to sit on his desk. She jumped up again immediately and rubbed her sore bottom. He helped her to sit on his lap and she found a place that didn't hurt so much.

"You understand what just happened?"

"Not exactly," she said.

"Something happened inside of you. You 'flew.' Do you understand the term?"

"No, but it does make sense."

"You now know that you were born to be a submissive—my submissive."

Emily slowly nodded. She could see that now. He had helped her along, guiding her, training her, until she finally admitted to herself what she really needed. Being tied up had merely clarified her understanding. Those orgasms were the proof. To go back to those days when the fumbling sex with a boyfriend gave her a tiny climax would be impossible now. Even as she admitted it, the idea terrified her.

"I'm scared," she whispered.

"I know you are. The door has been opened and you're afraid of what lies beyond. But know this—I will take care of you."

"You will?" After all, she reminded herself, he was the one pushing her into those dark corners of her own mind.

"Yes. Do you know how long I've been searching for a woman like you?"

A small smile came to her lips and she knew now why Mr. Caudry had gone through so many secretaries. He was looking for the perfect submissive.

"You don't need to be afraid."

She nodded.

"You must learn to trust me completely. Can you do that?"

"I-I think so, sir."

"Good." He reached past her and opened the desk drawer. "Do you know what day it is?"

"Friday, sir."

"Yes, but it's also pay day." He removed an envelope and handed it to her.

She clutched it to her chest. "Thank you, sir."

"Open it."

She fumbled with the flap and ripped it open. She took out the check and read the amount and a small frown flashed across her face. It was for exactly what Mrs. Dowd had promised her, no more. "Thanks," she said lamely.

"Were you expecting more?"

"Oh, no sir!" But she had been. Hadn't she gone above and beyond the job description?

"Wait." He eased her off his lap and she stood next to the desk, feeling her pussy hum its happy tune. She watched as he pulled his wallet from his pants pocket and opened it.

"Sir! You don't have to—"

"Shhh." She stopped immediately.

He fished out three hundred dollar bills and pressed them into her palm.

"Oh, sir, I can't—"

"Do you know what this makes you?"

"W-what?"

"Do you know what this makes you?"

She felt a burning sensation in her face. Her eyes met his and she knew what he was talking about. Her mouth opened to protest.

"No…"

"Yes. It makes you my little whore. My submissive. That's what you will become because that's what you need. Deep down." He tapped her chest and she knew he was right. How did he know that secret part of her?

"You understand? This paycheck is for the work you do to help the company. This money," he said, pointing at the bills in her damp hands, "is for all you'll be doing to please *me*."

She could only nod, not sure how she felt about it. Her mind was confused. She wanted to go away and think about, maybe ask Julie. Everything had been moving so fast.

"I don't know, sir…"

"Yes, you do know. You've known it since that first day I spanked you. If you didn't want it, you would've quit on the spot. Or reported me."

"Did other girls report you?"

"Yes, some did. Others simply quit."

"Didn't you get into trouble?" She could imagine angry lawyers storming the building.

"No. The girls were quietly paid off. The company won't risk what I bring in."

"So all this time, you've been looking?"

"Yes. And I've found her. You."

Emily felt pleased. Did this mean he would take her to live with him? Marry her? It was too bold a question to ask, so she didn't. But she could ask a related question.

"So what are my duties now?"

"To obey."

Emily shivered.

CHAPTER ELEVEN

Monday morning, Emily felt apprehension mixed with excitement as she waited for Mr. Caudry to arrive. Her life was going to be vastly different now and she wasn't sure if she was ready for it. But her pussy hummed contentedly, telling her just to go with it.

He came in, expressionless as usual. Did she expect a smile? No, that wasn't like him. He wasn't her boyfriend, she reminded herself; he was something else entirely. She wasn't even sure what. There was nothing in her life that gave her any frame of reference.

Emily followed him inside. He hadn't even had to tip his head. Already she was being conditioned. Her pussy moistened and her nipples hardened. She shut the door behind her and waited in front of his desk. He sat in his chair and gazed upon her.

"Take off your clothes."

She hesitated for only a second before her hands went to her blouse and she began to unbutton it. Shrugging it off her shoulders, she placed it on the chair next to her. Her bra followed, allowing her nipples to expand in the cool air. Next came her skirt and it pooled down around her ankles. Her red thong slipped down to join it. She stepped out, moving closer to his desk. At last, she kicked off her shoes.

He didn't say anything, he just stared at her, a slightly bemused expression on his face. Emily felt self-conscious but she didn't move or try to hide her body from him.

"Come for me," he said.

At first, she thought he said, "Come *to* me" and she started to move forward. Then she stopped and realized his exact words. Her mouth came open. A pink flush rose up across her chest to her neck and face. Her hand moved slowly down to the vee of her legs and she adjusted her stance. Her middle finger began to caress her pussy. She could feel the wetness there and she drew it up to her clit, which already was standing at attention.

She closed her eyes and her head tipped back as the pleasure ran through her. Her shoulders shook and she tried to forget that she was standing there like a slut, rubbing herself at his command.

"Ohhhhh." The first tendrils of her orgasm fluttered through her. Part of her feared she could not do this and another part worried she might fall down from the power of it. As she continued to stroke her pussy, her climax swelled and she could feel it now, closing in on her.

"Stop," he said and she groaned but obeyed. She opened her eyes to lock onto his.

"Lick your fingers."

Emily tasted herself. She smiled nervously at him and waited. She wanted to come and hoped he might demand she finish. How far she had come in just a few short days? Earlier, she would've been mortified to masturbate in front of him, now she was silently begging him to let her finish.

"Now, come here and give me my morning blowjob."

She fought her disappointment as she moved toward him and dropped to her knees by his chair. His cock was soon out and in her mouth. She sucked it and was rewarded by its hardness. He tasted good in her mouth. His cock belonged there, she thought. Just before he squirted, he suddenly pushed her head back and splashed his seed across her face and neck. She kept her mouth open, trying to catch it. She started to use her fingers to gather his seed so she could swallow it but he stayed her hand.

She stared, her eyes questioning him.

"Spread it over your tits and upper lip," he said. "I want you to feel it on you and smell it all day long."

She obeyed, torn between the excitement of this act of ownership and embarrassment to face her co-workers. Would they be able to smell it too? To see the sheen of it on her face? When she rubbed his seed over her breasts, she thought she might be able to climax from that alone.

"Good. You may get dressed."

She rose and returned to the center of the room and slowly dressed, her eyes on his. He smiled and watched. When she was slipping her thong up into place, he shook his head. She paused. He wiggled his fingers and she removed her panties and handed them over to him. He placed them on the corner of his desk, where anyone could see them.

She shivered.

"Now go get me a cup of coffee."

Emily went at once to obey.

As she walked among her co-workers, she looked at their expressions. Did she see the wrinkle of a nose? A questioning glance? Could they tell she was naked underneath her skirt? Could they smell his seed on her skin? It didn't matter if they did. Emily knew she was lost. No one could make her feel this way. She needed Mr. Caudry now. She was his whore.

She returned with the coffee and placed it on his desk, next to her wispy red panties.

"Thank you," he said and she smiled and withdrew.

J.W. MCKENNA

It was hard to concentrate on her work with the smell of him in her nose and her naked pussy weeping with need. He hadn't allowed her to come. Was she being punished? Or was he simply trying to catch up? Again, she had no say in it. That was up to him.

Mr. Caudry had to go out to meet with a client and Emily felt a sense of loss when he left. She went back to her letters and made two mistakes. Each one caused her bottom to twitch. She printed them out and placed them on his desk. Her stomach flip-flopped as she could imagine herself being punished for those careless errors. She wasn't even sure why she had done it.

At lunch, she slipped out to walk the streets, enjoying the feel of the air between her legs. She felt an urge to flash someone and resisted it. When she returned, Mr. Caudry was there. She went inside at once and closed the door.

His expression told her he found the mistakes. Without a word, Emily removed her skirt and placed herself over the desk, her ass up and ready.

"You did this on purpose, didn't you?"

She looked at him without expression. That was enough to tell him the truth.

"I can see that your punishments are going to have to change."

Emily felt confused. Didn't he enjoy spanking her?

"We have to move beyond the pain you've been experiencing and we can't do that here. Too noisy," he said, coming around the desk and pulling her upright. His hand went between her legs and she opened herself to him. Her eyes closed and she could feel her orgasm, the one he had denied her earlier, returning full force.

Once again he stopped and she moaned her frustrations.

"Bad girls don't get orgasms," he said. He picked up the letters and handed them to her. "We'll discuss your punishment later."

Emily put her skirt back on and went back to her desk, feeling unsettled. She made the corrections and brought the letters back to him. He read them over and nodded. "Much better." He called her over and reached underneath her skirt and gave her needy pussy a rub. He stopped before she could climb to her orgasm. "That will be all."

Damn it, she thought. *He's going to tease me all day!*

An hour later, Emily couldn't stand it and went to the restroom. In the stall, she brought herself to a quick climax, knowing it was forbidden but unable to stop herself. She had never been kept on edge like this before and she couldn't handle it.

When she returned, she tried to pretend nothing had happened. When Mr. Caudry called her in to dictate a letter as she sat on his lap, his fingers underneath her skirt, she tried to act like she was completely frustrated when he stopped.

He wasn't fooled.

"What's this?"

"What, sir?"

"You came, didn't you?"

"What? Oh, no…"

"Don't lie to me!" His normally calm voice took on an edge and she broke down.

"I'm sorry! I was just so needy! You've kept me on edge all day long!"

"That's right. That's where I want you to be! How dare you disobey me!" He pushed her off onto the rug. "Get out."

"Please, sir! I'm sorry. I won't do it again! Here, spank me! I'll be good."

Mr. Caudry took a deep breath. He grabbed a pad from his desk drawer and wrote something on it. "Very well. If you're truly sorry, you'll come to my house after work. Six o'clock sharp. Be on time or pack up your things and get out."

She left, trying not to cry in front of the other workers.

He ignored her the rest of the day, which only made her feel worse. She knew she was going to be punished tonight and she welcomed it. Anything to get back on his good side, to keep him in her life.

BOOK 2

Edward

CHAPTER TWELVE

Edward Caudry paced as he waited for Emily to arrive. Everything was working out perfectly, so why did he feel like disaster loomed around every corner? He had never met a woman like Emily before. He hardly dared admit she captivated him.

It certainly hadn't started that way. On her first day, he had dismissed her as yet another in a string of useless secretaries who would eventually disappoint him. But almost right away, he noticed something different about her. She was shy and respectful, yes, as most of them were at first. Yet underneath, he caught a glimpse of something deeper. When he pushed her, she responded with such ardent sensuality he began to wonder if she might be the submissive he craved.

Counselors would unite in their condemnation of his tactics as a boss, and Edward was well aware of his limitations. He tried to fight it, tried to separate his work life from his personal life—what little he had of one—but it proved to be impossible. With every new secretary, he was searching for another woman like Adriana.

Adriana had been the love of his life, five years ago. He had been a much more pleasant man to be around, for he had his beautiful submissive to please him. Together they explored their growing relationship, finding what worked for them and what did not. Truth be told, Edward was a bit of a conservative dominant, not really into the heavier aspects of the lifestyle. It was all foreplay, really. He and Adriana would play their games and make magnificent love afterward.

He had been foolish enough to think his version of "Dom-lite" was enough for her. And it had been, until they had visited that damn private club.

There they met Paul Antonelli. The bastard. He had come on all friendly and helpful, at first. Bought them drinks, gave his advice, acted like a gentleman. He made Adriana call him "Master Paul" and Edward had been intrigued and believed he could learn a lot from him.

So they began to visit Paul's estate and play some of his games with his other pretend sex slaves. It was all heady and exciting, having women around who would do just about anything for you. Edward did discover much about what a true submissive needs.

Yet it was Adriana who really learned, not him. Master Paul opened up a whole new world for her, a world that went far beyond Edward's tame version of the Dom/sub lifestyle. He had thought he was enough for her but he was wrong. Within two months, Adriana left him for Paul, telling Edward that her new master gave her what she had been searching for all her life.

"Please don't hate me, Edward," she said. "The heart wants what the heart wants."

It was all crap. How could a submissive choose her master? Wasn't he supposed to be in charge? He knew she would've stayed if he'd been a stricter Dom and given her what she craved. He let her go in a fit of anger and almost immediately regretted it. When he showed up at Paul's estate three days later, he really thought she might change her mind and return to him. What he saw, however, convinced him Adriana was lost to him forever.

When Paul had summoned her, he had been shocked. She had welts all over her body and her nipples and labia were already pierced. He couldn't imagine how she could allow herself to be treated this way. Yet her expression was one of devotion, of acceptance and, yes, love. She knelt before him, her eyes downcast and murmured, "How may I please you, sir?"

Edward looked from her to Paul and back again. Paul said to him, "She'll do anything you need—a blowjob, a fuck or, if you prefer, you may whip her. She loves to fly."

Edward didn't even understand what he meant, although he would soon learn all about "flying." He was shocked. It was quite clear that his version of "the life" barely touched the surface of what Adriana had sought. How could she do this to him?

The heart wants what the heart wants.

He ran stumbling out of the mansion, eyes filled with tears. He mourned her for a week and when the week was up, he never cried again. Nor had he dated. Instead, Edward threw himself into his work and soon rang up more sales than any other man or woman at Bonham Industries. He became so valuable, the company would do almost anything to please him. But they couldn't give him what he really needed.

Every secretary who crossed his path reminded him of Adriana in some way. He expected to be disappointed, and so he was. He expected they would leave, so he drove them away. He wasn't even sure why he was so cruel—did he really expect to find another woman like his former love? And if he did, wouldn't she just leave him again?

Yet from the first moment, Emily seemed different. She had intrigued him. He allowed himself a little hope. Perhaps in her, he might find a better fit. His greatest worry was she would become like Adriana in the end and require more than he could offer. That was why he paced now, nervously checking the clock and waiting for Emily to show up.

She didn't have to. He wouldn't fire her for not wanting to come to his house and thus, expand their relationship. But somehow, he knew she would.

And the thought both thrilled and worried him.

He poured himself another drink, a half this time. Don't lose control, he told himself. He wondered if Emily would have trouble finding the place. Should he have drawn her a map? He stopped, taking a deep breath. Stop acting like a fool! He would need to gain control of his emotions if this was to work.

He thought of Paul. It sickened him to remember the man, but it helped steel his resolve. In the next moment, he thought of Adriana and shook his head. *What a fucking mess*, he thought. *Get a grip!*

The doorbell rang. He glanced at the clock—straight up six. He put down the drink at once and stood. Edward imagined himself back at work, in control once more and he thrust back his shoulders. Taking another deep breath, he strode to the door and opened it.

Emily stood there, looking small and frightened. She still wore her work outfit, a blouse and skirt underneath a sweater against the chill. He wondered if she had put on new panties underneath.

"Come in," he said and stepped aside.

She scurried past him, her eyes downcast.

"Did you have trouble finding the place?" He led her into the living room where a fire crackled in the hearth.

"Yes sir, at first. But I figured it out eventually."

That told him she had left early to arrive on time.

Probably came directly from work, fearing she might be late and displease him.

"Good. Show me."

Emily's eyes jerked up to meet his and he stared at her. He knew what she was thinking: How would the relationship change, now that she was here, not protected by the work environment? Not that anything they had done in the office reflected a normal working relationship! But still—here she was vulnerable to anything, unless she bolted. He didn't want her to panic. He wanted to ease her into it.

"Well?"

Her hands went to her skirt and she raised the hem. He was pleased to see she had not put on new panties. Hers were still on the corner of his desk, something for her to focus her eyes on whenever she came inside. He imagined her pussy would already be wet. He nodded, pleased. She probably hadn't climaxed since her little transgression and now was clearly in a state.

He knew, at that moment, she fully expected to have sex with him. In fact, she probably welcomed it. She was already well on her way to become a wonderful submissive. The question that echoed in his mind, was he ready to risk becoming a real Dom again?

"Would you like a drink?"

The words startled Emily. She stared at him, her skirt still raised. Finally she nodded.

"What would you like?"

"Um, bourbon and water?"

He waved at her skirt and she let it fall. He went to the bar and fixed her a drink. When he brought it to her, she seemed enormously grateful and terrified at the same time.

"Relax. Sit," he said. "Don't be afraid." Gently he put his arm around her as he led her to the couch.

She sat nervously, her body stiff as she took a quick sip and coughed. Edward tried again.

"I understand this is new. You're my secretary and suddenly, here you are. You're probably wondering why I told you to come."

She stared at him. Then she lowered her eyes. "I disobeyed you." Her voice was almost inaudible.

"Yes, you did. And you will be punished. But I don't want you to worry too much." He paused, and added: "Truth is, you are quite valuable to me as a secretary. I would hate for your carelessness to ruin that."

Emily looked up, hope in her eyes. "I'm sorry, sir. I don't know why I made those mistakes."

"I think I know. You wanted the attention. You wanted to be punished. You need that."

She did not disagree. Why else would she make such silly mistakes? And sneaking off to the bathroom for a quick climax? She must really think she's in for it, he mused. What would happen next would have to be done carefully. He didn't want to scare her off, and yet he didn't want her to think he was anything less than a masterful Dom. Someone like Paul. He closed his eyes briefly and tried to push the man's face out of his mind.

He sipped at his drink, getting himself under control. This was not going the way he had planned it. Time to get back on track!

"Very well. Sip your drink while I explain." She took another healthy swig, her eyes never leaving his. He sat down across from her and gathered his thoughts. "At work, you've... uh, pleased me. But those mistakes you made on purpose require something extra. You need a place to be able to cry out, even beg."

Her eyes grew wide and he nodded. "Oh yes. Did you think you'd get away with a simple spanking in light of your willfulness?"

Emily grew pale.

"Clearly it's what you wanted. Or maybe needed," he said, enjoying the play of emotions across her face.

"Please don't hurt me," she whispered.

Edward recalled Adriana saying similar words to him, a long time ago. And he had listened and gone easy on her. He hadn't realized she had secretly wanted to be punished severely—in fact, she needed it. The protesting was part of her submission. That didn't mean she had wanted to be permanently marred, no. A good Dom would know exactly how far to push her—and now Edward had a good idea of what Emily was seeking.

Her inner submissive wanted to be able to let go and "fly"— oh, yes, he knew what the term meant by now. It described what a sub experienced during punishments. It required total trust between Dom and sub, for she would have to know in her heart he cared deeply for her and did not want to damage her. At the same time, she would want to experience a certain amount of fear too. It was a delicate balancing act.

"Remove your clothes," he said.

Emily's eyes widened for a moment and her hand shook when she put down her glass. She stood and shrugged off her sweater. Her hands went to her blouse. Her eyes remained on his as she unbuttoned it slowly, revealing her lacy bra. Edward smiled.

The blouse slipped off her shoulders and she placed it carefully over the chair. Her skirt followed and his smile broadened once more when he saw her nakedness. The bra was shrugged off and she stood there, watching him drink in her body.

"Are you wet?"

She blushed and looked away. Then she nodded imperceptibly.

"Show me."

Her eyes returned to his. Her fingers reached between her legs and she brought them up to show him the wetness there.

"You're excited by all this, aren't you?"

"Yes, sir," she said quietly.

"Let's see how excited you are after your punishment."

She shook as he stood and loomed over her. He took her hand and led her into the bedroom. When she saw the whip laid out on the four-poster bed, Edward felt her resistance and he pulled her into the room. She whimpered as he pushed her over the foot of the bed, her face right next to the whip. It was a cat o'nine tails, a collection of suede strips held by a black handle. Edward watched as her eyes grew wet. He knew she was truly afraid and had not yet learned to trust him.

He patted her back to comfort her and began tying her arms to the posts at the head of the bed with long straps, pulling her hips tight against the edge of the mattress. She struggled but did not really try to get away. He returned to the end of the bed and used more leather straps to tie her ankles to the posts, stretching her legs apart and exposing that most tender of flesh.

"Please, sir," she begged.

"You made those mistakes on purpose, did you not?"

She had no answer for that. Her mouth opened and closed.

"You asked for this." He picked up the whip and slashed it through the air a few times. Her eyes went wide but he could see a trust there. He nodded as if to reassure her. This was what separated the Doms from the pretenders, he thought. She needed this, but she was afraid. There was a fine line between the Doms and the abusers, he reminded himself. Watch her carefully! She must know she can trust you.

He moved into position and measured his swing. He wasn't sure just how hard to hit, this first time, so he gave her one quick strike across both cheeks.

"Owww!" She seemed to be more startled than afraid and that told him he was allowing her to let go and not worry about him losing control. He paused to admire the group of pink welts he had raised. Good. Not hard enough to break the skin, but hard enough to sting.

"What were we up to, anyway?" he inquired. "I think it was eight strokes per mistake, wasn't it?"

By her expression, he could see she had quite forgotten herself. It had been a while since he had counted strokes. He didn't really intend to give her sixteen, he just wanted her to feel his total control over her and know that she brought it on herself.

Whack! The second stroke caused another cry from Emily and she was wiggling her ass all around in an effort to cool it off. She looked so good, he wanted to take her, right then and there, but he resisted.

Whack!

"Oh my god! Please, Mr. Caudry!" she begged. "I'll do better!"

"Why, we've barely started, my dear."

Each strike left more welts and Edward was having trouble finding fresh skin to hit. Already she was marked from her upper thighs to the top of her peach-shaped ass and he knew he was about done. He watched her face to see if she was "flying," but she simply looked frightened and in pain.

Hmm, he thought. Maybe it takes a while to bring about her total capitulation so she could be released into the moment. Like Adriana did under Paul's lash, he remembered.

He struck her one more time, more to erase the memory in his head than to punish Emily further. She cried out and shook from head to foot. Her ass wiggled so naughtily, he dropped the whip and came forward. His fingers found the core of her and she was dripping wet. His cock grew rock hard.

"What's this?" he teased. "This makes you horny?"

"Please, Mr. Caudry, I'll do better, really. I promise." She was babbling.

"Shhh," he said. "Tell me why you're so wet."

He could see that flush rise across her upper body to her face. She rubbed her pussy against his fingers, willing to sacrifice her body if he would only stop whipping her. It was more than that, of course, he knew. She wanted to feel his hard cock thrusting into her but was too embarrassed to say it. That would be too forward for a sub to admit. She would want him to take control.

"I-I don't know..."

"Really? I think you secretly like it. Otherwise, you wouldn't have made those mistakes. You certainly knew I would punish you, although I doubt you thought it would be any more than a few swats with a ruler, right?"

She nodded, her face red.

"And now, look at you! All spread out and your ass well-marked, and yet, you're dripping wet! Tell me why, Emily."

"I...I..."

He waited her out. Finally, she said, "I n-need it."

Edward nodded. "Of course you do, my dear. And I'm well aware of it.'

He moved around to the side so she could watch him and unzipped his pants and slipped them off. His boxer shorts followed and his hard cock sprung free. "Look what you did to me, Emily," he said.

She stared at it and licked her lips.

"I'm going to continue with your punishment now."

"Noooo," she breathed. "Please, you can..." She couldn't say it.

"What was that?"

"You can...make love to me."

Edward smiled. "Make love. How quaint. You understand we have a new relationship, you and me. I fully intend to fuck you tonight, Emily. But first, you're going to fly again. I'm sure you can imagine what your orgasms will be like."

He began to hit her again, all over her reddened ass and she gasped and cried and begged him to stop. He ignored her, watching her carefully. Soon she stopped begging and just endured it. He stepped to the side for a moment and saw a blank expression on her face.

Her eyes closed and her breathing stilled. A look of utter peace descended over her features. It was poetry to watch her. She was flying.

He kept up the whipping, going softer now, for it wouldn't take much to keep her flying. Finally, he gauged she'd had enough and tossed the whip to the ground. He came close to her, one hand on her back and gently stroked her soft skin until her eyes refocused.

"There, now you know what flying is."

She could only gasp in response.

"I'm going to fuck you now. You understand when you feel my cock in your wet pussy that this will signify you giving over yourself to me. This won't be anything like any relationship you've had before. I will always be your boss and you will always be my subordinate. Do you understand?"

She nodded, her eyes drifted down to fasten on his erection.

"We won't be 'making love' or any of that nonsense. I'm not your boyfriend. You will be my fuck-toy, my sex slave. Your job will be to bring me pleasure and to obey. Do you understand?"

She nodded again and her eyes rose to lock onto his, perhaps to measure the depth of his convictions.

"So tell me again, what do you want, my little slut?"

"F-fuck me," she said, giving up what little power she still had. She would be his now.

"Good girl. Now, tell me, are you on the pill?"

Emily shook her head.

"Why not?"

"I don't have a...a boyfriend." She seemed embarrassed by the fact.

"I'm surprised. You're such a pretty girl."

She just closed her eyes.

"Or maybe no one could really give you what you wanted, deep down. Is that right?"

Emily opened her eyes and stared at him. Then she nodded, ever so slightly.

"I'll bet you weren't sure yourself what you really wanted, is that right? Until you came to work for me."

She nodded again.

Edward went to the nightstand and pulled out a condom. "I'll wear a condom tonight. When is your period?"

Her face flushed pink. "Uh, next week."

"Good. I'm going to start fucking you without a condom in a month. That should give you plenty of time to protect yourself."

He went around behind her and slipped the condom on. His fingers teased her until she was gasping, then he thrust into her all at once, his hips touching her tortured flesh. Emily moaned and came immediately. Her body shook with the power of it.

Edward kept stroking and felt her rising quickly to another climax. He enjoyed watching her writhe, her body caught between pleasure and pain. He was sure, up until this moment, she hadn't really been able to articulate what had been missing in her life. Now she would know.

His strokes increased and Emily began making noises in her throat as the orgasms rolled over her. She gripped the leather straps holding her and pulled back on them, making her body taut as the sensations rocketed through her.

"Ohgodohgodohgodohgod!" she cried out, lifting her upper body off the mattress.

Edward came hard inside her and it pushed her over the edge into a final, powerful climax. She collapsed onto the bed, sweat beading on her back and face. Edward wondered if she had ever had an orgasm like it before.

He slipped out of her and untied her. Climbing up onto the bed, he held her face in his lap, stroking her hair and telling her how good she had been. She smiled and lay limp, unable to move.

At last, the strength returned to her body and she groaned.

"Hurts, huh?"

"Yeah." She reached back and just barely touched her ass and winced.

"I've got something to put on it." He went into the bathroom and found the tube of ointment. When he spread it on, she jerked once and settled in.

"Is that better?"

"Yessss," she moaned. "Much."

He left her there and went to make them new drinks. She took hers gratefully and propped herself up on one elbow and sipped at it. For several minutes, nothing was said. She was still naked, he was still dressed only in his shirt, but neither one was embarrassed.

The color returned to her cheeks and he took the empty glass and set it on the nightstand.

"I trust we'll have no more mistakes, hmmm?" He smiled and winked.

"Oh, no sir," she said at once.

"Good. Then I'll see you Monday morning, bright and early?"

"Yes sir." She eased herself off the bed and went into the living room. She found her clothes and began putting them on. He watched from the hallway, sipping the rest of his cocktail.

When she was finished, she turned and looked at him. He realized she needed some reassurance. He raised his glass. "You are, by far, my favorite secretary."

She smiled shyly and disappeared into the night.

Edward sat down heavily onto his chair. He pressed the cold glass against his forehead.

"That went well," he breathed.

120

CHAPTER THIRTEEN

Monday morning, Emily was in her place by his door, waiting. He nodded at her as he went by and she followed him into his office. He put his briefcase down and turned toward her.

"Good morning," he said and raised an eyebrow at her.

Emily lifted her skirt at once, showing him a pair of sexy bikini panties. He nodded. "Very nice. Please remove them."

Her eyes went wide for a moment before she obeyed. Her skirt dropped and she reached underneath to pull her panties down. She handed them over but he just pointed to the corner of the desk. She saw her red thong panties were still there from last week. Her fingers opened and she added her new panties to the pile.

Edward smiled. She was beginning to get the picture.

"Show me your ass."

She lifted her skirt and turned around. The welts had faded but were still faintly visible. Just looking at them made him hard.

"I'd like some coffee, please."

She dropped her skirt and left at once. He began whistling as he fired up his computer. He checked his email and looked up a few minutes later when Emily returned, a coffee mug in hand. She placed it in front of him and waited.

"That will be all."

Emily left, confusion on her face. He smiled, knowing she was wondering why he didn't want his morning blowjob. He had other plans. It was time to make her realize just how much control he had over her life.

Edward spent the next half-hour answering emails and setting up appointments. Finally, he rose and went out to Emily's desk and stood close. She looked up, expectantly.

"Your skirt. Give it to me."

She blanched white. Her eyes went to the cubicle farm just beyond her area, separated only by her desk and that small section of plywood. He could see her mind working—if she lost her skirt, she would be trapped at her desk, unable to move.

"I don't have all day, Miss Robinson," he barked.

Her hands went to her waist and she fumbled for the button. It wasn't easy for her to unzip it and wiggle it off her hips, but she did it quickly. She thrust the garment into his hands. He took it and went back into his office and shut it into his briefcase. He wished he could see her expression as she sat there, naked from the waist down. He could bet her legs were tightly closed and she was scooted all the way up against the edge.

Edward had a luncheon appointment out of the office, so he worked until eleven-thirty before he went out into Emily's station. She was flush with embarrassment and her eyes pleaded with him.

"I have to go out for a while. Will you be all right until I get back?"

"Sir! No, please," she whispered. "I...I..."

"I'll only be gone an hour, maybe an hour-and-a-half."

"Please, sir! I have to go to the bathroom!" she whispered urgently.

"Oh. I don't suppose you could hold it?"

"No! Please, sir!"

"Does this mean I can expect excellent work from now on?"

"Yes, sir! I promise!"

"Very well." He opened his briefcase and dumped her skirt onto her desk. Without another word, he left.

When he returned, she was typing up a letter. He nodded at her and she followed him inside. "I'd like that blowjob now," he said.

She dropped to her knees in by his chair.

"No, I'd like you to be naked. It stimulates me."

Emily made no complaint. She rose quickly and stripped off her clothes. Edward leaned back in his chair and watched how eagerly she obeyed. She clearly didn't want another session like she had experienced that morning!

Just having her naked body so close to him make him want to fuck her all over again. But that wouldn't be proper in the workplace. He laughed to himself even as he thought it. Like what they were doing was!

Her technique had improved over the last few days. Or maybe it was just that she was so anxious to please him. Either way, she soon had his seed boiling and he grabbed her head and erupted into her throat. She swallowed quickly and smiled as she zipped him up.

She stood and picked up her skirt.

"Wait," he said and she stopped, her eyes questioning him.

"Come here."

He could see she thought he was going to fuck her, although he was quite satisfied. He made her straddle his knees. He held her close and stroked her back, feeling her shiver under his touch. With his other hand, he rubbed her wet pussy until she was gasping before he pulled away. She stood, her hips shaking and waited for him to continue, but when he didn't, she stepped back and picked up her bra.

"Put the bra on the desk."

Her eyes went wide but she obeyed. Her little pile of undergarments was growing. The blouse wasn't see-through, but her darker nipples did show through. She looked down at herself and blushed once more.

"Sir..." she began.

"That will be all, Emily."

She pulled up her skirt and left, her head hanging low.

She returned an hour later with some letters. He made her stand by his desk and he reached under her skirt and stroked her bare bottom while he read them. Occasionally, his fingers would stray to her pussy and note how wet she was. She gasped and moved her legs apart, encouraging him, but he didn't allow her to come.

"Excellent," he said at last. "Not a single mistake."

"Yes, sir."

"That will be all."

She left, clearly frustrated.

By five, he could tell she was anxious to unlock the secret that would allow her release. He could imagine her thinking she had done everything he had asked—so why wouldn't he let her come?

"Sir?"

"Yes, Emily?"

"Uh, I was wondering..."

"Yes?" he said impatiently.

She paled at his stern demeanor. "Well, sir, I wanted to ask if I may...uh..."

"Spit it out, please, I have to go."

"Come," she said, her face reddening.

"Come?" He pretended not to understand.

"Uh, I've been on edge all day! Usually you let me come... you know..."

"Ah, I see." He snapped his briefcase closed. "Not today, Emily. Consider it a lesson. When you make deliberate mistakes just to get attention, you must understand how much that disappoints me."

"But you punished me already!"

"Did I? I never said I was finished." He paused. "However, if you obey me now and don't come all night, we can start fresh tomorrow. All right?"

She lowered her head and nodded. He wasn't fooled. He could guess she was thinking: *How will he know what I do at home alone?*

"Very well. See you then." He picked up his briefcase and left her standing there.

That night, he called her at home. She sounded startled to hear his voice. "Mr. Caudry!" she said. "What...what..."

"I'm calling to check on you, my dear. Have you been good?"

"What? Oh, yes..." She seemed flustered.

"You haven't allowed yourself to touch your wet pussy?" he pressed.

"No! Uh, no sir..."

"I would be very disappointed if you did."

"Yes sir! I haven't, sir!"

He wasn't sure if she was telling the truth but it really didn't matter. He wanted to let her know he was thinking about her. It was his way of telling her how much she meant to him. He hoped she'd understand that. "Good girl. See you tomorrow." He hung up.

The next morning, he invited Emily into his office and made her lift her dark blue skirt. She wore no panties this time.

"Good," he said, pleased. He motioned her forward and ran a finger along her cleft. She jumped. She was wet already—or maybe she was still wet from yesterday. Either way, it was a good sign.

"Now the blouse."

Her fingers fumbled with her buttons and as they parted, Edward could see her cotton bra underneath. He shook his head and pointed to the pile of her undergarments on the corner of the desk. Her mouth opened and closed and he thought she might protest. She shrugged off her blouse and unhooked her bra and let it slide down her arms onto the desk. Quickly she buttoned up her light blue blouse and stood there, her eyes on the rug.

He could see just a pale outline of her nipples through the material. "Do we understand each other now?"

She nodded.

"You may go."

She fled, hunching her shoulders. Edward smiled and swept the pile of undergarments into a drawer. He would give those back to her later, once she had been thoroughly conditioned. Emily was already well on the way. He expected no more mistakes, but secretly hoped she would make some, just so he could push her further into the mindset he desired for her: Unquestioned obedience.

Emily came in with two letters, her shoulders still hunched, and he scanned them carefully. No mistakes. He nodded his acceptance and she started to leave.

"Emily."

She turned, expectantly.

"Don't hunch. Put your shoulders back."

She straightened up and he could see her nipples pressing against the material like headlights. He smiled and nodded. "Better."

She left quickly, her eyes downcast.

Edward had several appointments out of the office that afternoon and wasn't able to return until nearly five. He had done well and felt randy. He nodded at Emily and she came in behind him.

"Clothes," he said.

She stripped. There wasn't much covering her now—just a blouse and skirt. She kicked off her shoes and stood naked and flatfooted in front of the desk.

"I need a quick blowjob," he said.

She came around and dropped to her knees. She eased his cock out and dove on it. By now, she knew what he liked and he sat back and allowed it to happen. When he came inside her throat, she swallowed, never allowing a drop to escape. She peered up at him, waiting.

"Good girl," he said. "You've become an excellent secretary. Now, as I promised, you may come. Here, lean against my desk."

She stood there, expectantly. He knew she assumed he would touch her or fuck her, but he said nothing for a few seconds. Then: "You may begin.'

Emily's mouth dropped open. "Sir?"

"I said, you may begin. You wanted to come, didn't you?"

"Uh, yes, sir, but—"

"You'd prefer not to come?"

"No! I want to, but..."

He shook his head and said, "Very well. If you're too embarrassed, then you may go. Just don't touch yourself this evening."

"No! I want to!" Her hand went to her pussy and began to rub. He sat and watched her. Under his gaze, she had trouble reaching that tipping point. He wasn't going to let her off the hook. Then he saw something change in her eyes and they seemed to glaze over. That was good, for it showed she could let herself go. Within a minute, she was shaking with her release.

"Good girl," he said when she was done.

She sagged against his desk, her pussy and fingers wet. She sucked in a breath and tipped her head at her clothes. He nodded and she put them back on. She headed for the door.

"Emily."

She turned, her mouth half opened.

"Tonight, just before you eat, I want you to call and tell me what you're having."

Emily's face registered her confusion. "Sir?"

"You have my cell phone number, right?"

"Uh, yes, sir."

"Good." He turned to his computer, dismissing her. He did not look up when she left.

At home, while he was sipping a cocktail, his phone rang. He picked it up. "Yes?"

"Uh, Mr. Caudry, sir. I'm about to have, uh, a salad and a TV dinner."

"Really? A TV dinner? That's not acceptable."

"What? What do you mean?"

"Those things are full of fat and salt. I want you to take better care of your body, all right?"

"But sir! It's a low-cal dinner!"

"Are you arguing with me?"

"No, sir."

"Eat the salad. Throw away the dinner. Start to eat more healthy foods. Oh, you'd better not masturbate tonight." He hung up before she could protest. He sipped his drink, imagining Emily at home, staring at her TV dinner. Would she eat it in defiance of him? Would she touch herself, later in bed? He'd never know either way. He just wanted her to feel his presence in her life away from the office.

He wanted to own her.

Wednesday morning, Emily stood in front of his desk, her dark brown dress unbuttoned all the way down, showing that she was wearing no underwear. He nodded and yet he wasn't pleased. "I don't like those dark colors."

"Sir?" She looked down at her dress.

"I prefer lighter colors. Summer colors, if you will."

Emily stared at him and he knew what she was thinking: Lighter colors would show everyone she was naked underneath. She began to shake.

"Sir..."

"Are you questioning me?"

"No, sir, it's just that..."

"I'd like my blowjob now."

She came around his desk, confusion on her face, and yet he noted how quick she had been to obey. "Wait," he said. He pointed to her dress.

She blushed and stood. In one movement, she pulled it off her body and tossed it to the side. She bent down and unzipped him and soon was sucking eagerly on his cock. He came in her mouth and she stood. It had become routine now.

Emily waited, her eyes on his.

"Very well," he said. It was time for a reward. "Come here."

She stepped forward and he pushed her back until her hips met his desk. He helped her up until she was sitting, naked, her legs splayed out. He stroked her breasts and her head tipped back. She gave a low moan in her throat. His hand went to her bare pussy and felt the wetness within. He wondered if she had masturbated again last night. He rubbed her gently, stopping now and then to allow her orgasm to build within her.

"You've been a good girl," he whispered. "I'm very pleased."

She groaned and her hips began to shake. He watched as she climbed higher and higher toward her release and suddenly she grabbed at his arms and closed her legs against his hand. He enjoyed seeing her climax. Emily fell forward and rested her head on his shoulder.

"That will be all for now," he said.

She got to her feet and slipped on her dress. Her eyes were glazed and she moved in slow motion to the door.

"Emily."

She turned, blinking.

"I'd like a cup of coffee please."

She nodded and was gone. When she returned, he pretended nothing had happened between them. He was simply her boss, nothing more. She put his coffee down and waited for some sign from him, some acknowledgement of her existence. He glanced up. "That will be all."

She fled, confusion on her face.

Edward wasn't sure if he was acting like a proper Dom, although it felt that way to him. Being a novice worried him a little. He thought he could learn on the job as it seemed clear to him that Emily was an eager pupil. At least she seemed under his spell.

However, at this stage of their relationship, he was unsure of where to take it. No, that wasn't true—he knew how he'd like it to end: With her as his submissive at home, not at work. His confusion lay with how to get there. He supposed he could just demand she move in with him, but that seemed forced and premature. Still, he would have to push her further. Staying still wasn't an option either. Once again, he wondered what Paul would do in this situation. That led to wondering what Adriana was doing now and his thoughts turned dark.

Damn it.

Edward checked his watch and noted it was time to go. Lots of appointments, lots of money to be made. He left, telling Emily he wouldn't be back in the office today. A sudden thought occurred to him and he leaned close and said, "But I'd like you to call me on my cell to get permission to go to the restroom."

She stared, agape. "What?"

"You heard me. I want you to call first."

He left her there, mouth open, and walked toward the elevator, pleased with himself.

Two hours later, just after he had concluded a negotiation with a new client, his phone rang. He smiled when he noted it was from Emily. He excused himself from the man's office and went into the corridor.

"Yes?"

"Uh, sir?" Emily sounded stressed.

"Yes?" He allowed impatience to show in his voice.

"Um, I, uh, have to go."

"That isn't what I asked you to do, is it?"

131

"N-no, sir." She took a deep breath. "Sir, may I, er, go to the restroom?"

Edward looked around to make sure no one was listening. "How badly do you have to go?"

"Uh, real bad, sir. Please."

"Call me again in a half-hour," he said abruptly and hung up. He stared at the phone, half expecting it to ring again, but it didn't. He put the phone away and headed for his next meeting.

Edward was in the client's waiting room when his phone rang again, precisely thirty minutes later. He was pleased.

"Hello?"

"Sir! Please!" She sounded desperate.

"Oh, it's you." He glanced up to see the receptionist eying him. He stood and went into the corridor. "Yes?"

"Mr. Caudry! Please, I have to go!"

"Is that how we ask?"

"Uh, no sir. Uh, Mr. Caudry, please may I go to the restroom?"

"How do I know you won't masturbate while you're in there?"

"I promise!"

"Tell you what. You may go, but take your cell phone with you. Call me back as soon as you're inside, but before you go." He hung up.

He poked his head inside the client's office and told the secretary. "I'll be right out here when Mr. Billings is ready. I just have an issue at the office I need to clear up."

She nodded and he ducked back outside.

His phone rang and he answered it.

"I'm inside, sir!"

"Very well. Go into the stall and take off your dress."

"All the way off?"

"Yes," he said, pretending to be annoyed. He heard her fumble and then her voice came back. "I'm, I'm naked sir."

"Good. You may pee, but I want to hear it."

Edward could imagine her holding the phone between her legs for he suddenly heard a rush of water. Then her voice came back. "Sir? I did it."

"That's all you have to say?"

"Uh, thank you, sir?"

"That's better. Now clean up and get dressed. Don't stay in the restroom any longer than a minute or two or I'm afraid you might succumb to temptation."

He hung up and returned to the waiting area, a slight smile on his face.

CHAPTER FOURTEEN

The power was going to his head. He realized it and yet it was hard to stop himself. To have a true submissive at his beck and call inflated his ego and gave him a new energy. What next, he wondered? How could he push her further along until she agreed to come live with him and be his full-time slave—until she begged for it?

The word stopped him. "Slave" didn't feel right somehow. Submissive, yes, but slave? Edward wasn't sure. Damn, he wished he had a better feel for being a Dom. He certainly enjoyed it, and yet, it wasn't the way he'd been raised. His father had been a stern man and definitely ruled the family home. His mother took care of Edward and his brother Tim and that had been enough for her. The family unit worked well back then.

He wanted a similar life for himself. That would explain why, at age thirty-nine, he was still unmarried. He just hadn't found the right woman—until Adriana. Seeing how she enjoyed being submissive had awakened something within him. He could never go back after that.

And yet, he still had doubts. He felt like a blind man, stumbling around, trying to find his way in this unfamiliar landscape, driven only by his emotions and his instincts. Well, his instincts had served him well so far, so relax, he told himself. Besides, he truly liked Emily and wanted to protect her. That made a lot of difference.

When he arrived at the office Thursday morning, he noted with pleasure Emily had worn a light pink skirt and a white top. She had her shoulders hunched but he could still see the barest shadow of her nipples against her blouse. He nodded and she followed him into his office.

This time he didn't speak; he simply waited. Emily bit her lip but she lifted her skirt and showed him she wasn't wearing any panties.

"I'm pleased to see you aren't wearing a bra, either," he said.

She nodded, her eyes downcast.

"But I'm still displeased," he continued, watching how her eyes darted up to his face. "Last night, you failed to call about either your meals or your bathroom breaks."

Her mouth dropped open. "You mean..." She dropped the hem of her skirt.

"Yes. Wasn't I clear? I want you to call me and ask permission. What did you eat last night?"

"Uh...A TV dinner and a glass of wine."

"There, you see? I said those aren't good for you. I want you to eat healthy food from now on." He reached into his desk and pulled out his ruler. Her eyes locked onto it.

He stood and she immediately bent herself over the desk, bottom up.

Edward shook his head. "No, my dear. I want you to get completely undressed, remember?'

He turned on the radio and gazed at her as she fumbled out of her clothes, her hands shaking. Watching her get back into position, her cute ass up and ready for him, made him hard. He wanted nothing more than to plunge into her. It took will power to stop himself.

He gave her ten quick swats with the ruler. He could see the swats didn't hurt her as much as they made her wet. She was being conditioned nicely. Emily crouched over the desk, her ass wiggling invitingly. He guessed she wanted to be fucked but it wasn't time yet. It was good to make her wait—all the more eagerly she would accept his dominance of her.

"You may get dressed."

Emily rose quietly, her eyes on his, practically begging him to give her release. He turned to his computer and began to work. As she left, he said, "Bring me some coffee, will you?"

Edward didn't look up with she returned with his coffee a few minutes later. He sipped at it, pleased with himself. He imagined Emily walking to the break room, her nipples poking the front of her blouse, as other employees stared. It made him hard all over again, just thinking about it. Not that he wanted to share her with the office, but somehow, knowing she was on display delighted him.

An hour later, his intercom buzzed. "Yes?"

"Sir," he heard her whisper over the phone. "Uh, sir, I have to go."

"Go? Where?" He smiled to himself.

"No, I mean, please, sir, may I go?"

"You really must be clear, Emily."

He could hear the exasperation in her voice. "Sir, may I please go to the bathroom?"

"Yes, you may. But don't touch yourself."

"No, no sir."

At lunchtime, Edward left his office and stood by Emily's desk. She looked up, fear warring with lust in her eyes.

"Give me your skirt," he said.

"Sir! Please, not again!"

"Are you arguing with me? That will cost you."

"But sir, it's so embarrassing!"

He sighed. She wasn't doing very well.

"Come into my office."

She followed him inside. He shut the door behind her. "Take off your clothes."

She may have expected a quick spanking, but what he did next clearly surprised her. He picked up her skirt and blouse and stuffed them into his briefcase. He added her pile of undergarments from his desk drawer. Before she could protest, he left, closing the door behind him. He imagined her standing there naked, wondering if someone might come by to drop off something. Edward left, whistling to himself.

When he returned, forty minutes later, he came in to find Emily hiding behind his desk. He guessed she had been there the entire time, using the desk as a shield in case someone came by. When she saw him, she bolted to her feet, a look of relief on her face.

He raised a finger. "Oh, that's right," he said as if he had completely forgotten about her. He put his briefcase on the desk and opened it. There was nothing inside but papers.

"Oh, I'm sorry—I must've left them in my car. I'll get them later."

Her expression was priceless. "But sir!"

He went around and sat down. Emily moved aside, covering herself with her hands. "But sir!" she repeated.

"Yes?"

"I can't work like this!"

"No, I guess you can't." He opened his calendar on the computer and began entering appointments for later.

"Sir, what am I supposed to do?"

"I suggest when your boss gives you an order, you should obey it."

Emily stood there, mouth opening and closing, still trying to hide behind her hands. When Edward continued to ignore her, she sidled over to sit on the edge of the chair. When he glanced up a few minutes later, she was hunched over, her face red.

For the next hour, he pretended to ignore her as he made phone calls and tapped on his keyboard. At one point, Edward tossed some old files into the trash can by his desk. She never moved and her eyes never left his face, although he wouldn't acknowledge her. Finally, she spoke up.

"Sir. Uh..."

"Yes, Emily?"

"I, uh, have to go again."

"Is that how you've been taught to ask?"

"No, sir. May I go to the bathroom?"

"Of course you may, dear." He turned back to his computer.

"But sir! I need my clothes!"

"Yes, I can see that. But I'm busy now—I don't have time to fetch your clothes." He picked up his empty coffee cup. "I suppose I have to get my own coffee now, too, huh?"

He rose and moved past her toward the door. She gave a tiny screech when he opened it and he turned to find she had scrambled behind the side of the desk. He took his cup and left, leaving the door ajar behind him.

He took his time getting coffee. He smiled and chatted with a few other employees, some of whom seemed surprised to find Caustic Caudry chatting them up. When Mrs. Dowd came in, he made a point of asking her about her day.

"Oh, it's just fine, Mr. Caudry," she said, caught off guard at his friendly demeanor. "And you?"

"I'm having a good week, Doris."

"Well, good." She paused. "Uh, how's that new administrative assistant working out?"

From her expression, Edward guessed she was expecting another bad review, which would mean she'd have to find another poor victim for him.

"I am cautiously optimistic," he said, surprising her. "But it's still too early to tell."

"Oh, that's good! I'm so glad. It's been hard—" She stopped, as if she suddenly realized how that might sound. "I mean, the balance of personalities is always critical to a successful relationship."

"Yes, quite." He nodded and refilled his cup. Waving goodbye, he headed back to his office. The door was still ajar— Emily hadn't mustered up the nerve to close it. He sat at her desk for a few minutes, making another appointment. He knew she could hear him out there and it must've been torturous.

When he finally came in, she was huddled down by his desk, a look of desperation on her face. "Please, Mr. Caudry! I can't hold it anymore."

He found an empty vase on a shelf and handed it to her. She took it, eyes growing wide. "Here." He sat down and started making phone calls. Pitching his company's products often took a long time, for he had to chat up the client, asking about their work and families, before he could get to the nitty-gritty about why they should buy from him. Emily didn't dare interrupt. The longer he talked, the greener she became.

When she suddenly squatted down in front of his desk, he stood, the phone still pressed to his ear, and watched as she peed noisily into the vase, holding the wide mouth up carefully to catch every drop. He felt his cock grow hard at once.

"Yes, next Tuesday would be fine," he said to the client. "Say two p.m.? Great." He hung up.

Emily was bright red. She caught him looking at her and couldn't bear it. She was still hunched over, the last drops of pee dribbling into the vase. She looked around and didn't find anything to wipe with, so she just stood, holding the vase in one hand, a stunned expression on her face.

Edward watched her, saying nothing. She stared back, not able to speak. For a long time, they were frozen in an erotic tableau. Finally, he reached into his desk drawer and pulled out a tissue and handed it over. She accepted it, her face red. He watched as she dabbed at herself and tossed the tissue into the trash.

"I want a blowjob," Edward said. He sat down again.

Emily carefully put the vase down on a counter and came to him. She didn't complain as she took out his cock and he was pleased. She seemed to have broken through a barrier. For several minutes, he enjoyed her ministrations before erupting into her mouth.

"Thank you," he said as he zipped up. "That will be all."

"Sir!"

"Oh, right." He glanced at his watch. It was after three. "Very well. You'll be all right here until I get back?"

"Please hurry, sir!"

He got up and took his briefcase with him. He went down to the parking lot and began putting Emily's clothes into his case when he paused. A wicked thought occurred to him. He slipped behind the wheel of his car and fired it up. He turned off his cell phone before he reached the street and took the long way home, driving over the bridge across the bay, enjoying the scenery.

Once home, his phone rang several times, but he didn't answer it. He imagined Emily hunched down in his office, naked and terrified, and it made him feel powerful. But as the hours went on, doubts crept in.

How was this supposed to make her obedient, when she can't trust him?

Won't this make her simply afraid of him?

And finally: What if something were to happen to her?

"Aw, shit," he said and grabbed his car keys. Driving back to the office, he checked his watch. Six-thirty. She had been alone for three hours or so. He turned on his cell phone and noticed he had four messages. All were from Emily and all were about the same: "Sir! I'm trapped in your office! Help me! Please pick up! Please come back!"

He felt like a jerk and he increased his speed. It's not easy being a Dom, he thought. There's too much temptation to take things too far. She could be in real trouble! He parked at a meter in front of the building and raced inside, past the startled security guard.

"Mr. Caudry? Is everything all right?"

"Yes, Clarence. I just need to pick up something I forgot." He went upstairs to the darkened offices. He noted Emily's desk light was still on but the lights in his office were dark. He pushed open the door.

"Emily?"

Silence.

He went around the desk, looking for her, but she wasn't there. He went to the door and flipped on the lights, looking all around, as if he expected her to pop up from somewhere. Somehow, she had found some clothes and left, probably furious and hurt. But how? His eyes drifted down to his wastebasket, which he remembered dumping several old files in it that afternoon.

Now it was empty.

Oh shit. The janitors! He checked all the offices and found no one. He went down a flight of stairs and found two men on the next floor. One was wearing the standard dark blue shirt and pants that he'd seen many times when he worked late, but the other, a tall, broad-shouldered man, was missing his shirt. Edward went to him at once.

The man winked at him and said, "Hey, you must be lookin' for sumthin', huh?" He laughed and the other man stopped worked to laugh along with him.

Edward grimaced. "Yeah, uh, it was a good joke, wasn't it?"

"I tell ya, if'n I had a piece like that under my desk, why I wouldn't leave her alone, nuh uh!"

"Uh, what happened to her?"

"Oh, she begged me for my shirt. How could I refuse?"

"You gave her your shirt?" Edward could see it would've been enough to cover her.

"Well, I didn' exactly give it to her," he laughed and Edward felt his anger rising.

Edward's anger rose quickly. "What? What did you do?"

"Why, whadaya think? I made her buy it from me." He laughed again and the other man began to move closer, big grin on his face. Edward noted the name on his shirt: Ben.

"What do you mean, 'buy it from me'?"

"What do you think I mean? Naked little piece of ass like that?"

Edward wanted to hit him and realized not only would that be foolish, but he would be hitting the wrong person. If anyone deserved a punch in the nose, it was him.

"You—you...raped her?"

"Oh, hell no, man! She seemed ready to scream bloody murder! Once I got her calmed down, she agreed to trade me a BJ for my shirt. Then Ben showed up and he wanted a littl' sumtin' too..." He winked.

Edward had a vision of Emily, naked and on her knees, giving blowjobs to the two janitors. He clenched his fists.

"So what happened to her?" His anger was evident on his face.

Ben, an older man with a shock of white in his black hair, spoke up. "Hey, man, we didn't do nuthin' else to her. She was willin'."

"Yeah, she tol' us her boss made her do that," the shirtless janitor said. "You must be him, huh? That prolly won't look too good if it gets out."

"I just want to make sure she's all right."

"I dunno. After she was done with us, she put on Charlie's shirt and split," Ben said, jerking his thumb over his shoulder at his partner.

"I'll be checking with her to make sure nothing else happened to her," he said warningly, but it was an empty threat and both men knew it.

"Oh, sure, you check with your naked slut and see if she wants to press charges," Ben laughed. "I'm sure she'd like to forget the whole thing!"

Edward ran back upstairs and checked Emily's desk. Her purse was missing. That meant she probably made it to her car and drove home. He realized he didn't know where she lived. He dialed her cell phone and listened to it ring and ring. When it went to voice mail, he said, "Emily. It's me. I'm sorry. I don't know what got into me. I'm at the office and I found out what happened. Please call me."

He drove home, dispirited. He knew, without even thinking about it, that this was not something a Dom would do. Putting one's sub at risk like that was a boneheaded play. It had seemed so harmless, to leave her trapped naked in his office for a few hours. But it had been a big mistake.

He drove home and paced, waiting for her call. When it didn't come, he called again, but hung up when he got voice mail. She was probably furious and he couldn't blame her.

"Damn it," he said aloud.

CHAPTER FIFTEEN

The next morning, Edward trudged into his office. He had hoped by some miracle that Emily would be sitting at her desk as if nothing had happened, but wasn't surprised at all to see her desk empty.

He went inside and called her home number again. Still no answer. He had called her home and cell number several times last night and had gotten nowhere. Biting his lip, he called Mrs. Dowd. He was about to lie to the stern-faced HR director.

"Hi, Mrs. Dowd," he said, trying to put some cheer into his voice. He hoped she hadn't heard anything about last night's debacle.

"Oh, Mr. Caudry, I was about to call you," she said. He heard nervousness in her voice and his heart sank.

"Oh?"

"Yes, I got a call left on my voice mail this morning. Seems Ms. Robinson has quit. That was rather sudden, wasn't it?"

Edward closed his eyes. "Uh, yeah. I was calling to find out why she wasn't in. Um, did she give a reason?"

"Well...she said she'd had enough—I'm sure that you're familiar with that kind of explanation." Her voice had a scolding tone.

She assumed Emily grew tired of Mr. Caudry being a caustic, demanding boss and had quit to get as far away from him as possible. He did not dissuade her in her view.

"Well, that's disappointing," he said.

"Yes, it is. Do you know that's the sixth secretary who's left your office in the last two years?"

"That many, huh?"

"Yes. Perhaps you need to go a little easier on them."

"Well, I'm disappointed too. Emily was starting to work out."

"So you said. But her actions are telling quite a different story, aren't they?"

"Do you have her address? I'd like to go talk to her?"

"To what end?"

"To see if I can convince her to return to work."

"Do you really think that's wise?"

"Why not?"

"She might consider it some form of harassment."

"I doubt that. I'm just going to see if we can't work something out. She really was the most impressive of all my secretaries."

Mrs. Dowd's voice paused on the other end of the line. "Really?"

"Yes. Really."

"Well, it is a bit unusual..." He heard her fumbling around. "Here it is. Three-four-oh-six Maple Street. Apartment four-oh-five. Now you be nice. If she doesn't want to come back, don't yell at her."

"I won't, Mrs. Dowd," he said, closing his eyes.

He picked up his keys and returned to his car. It took him fifteen minutes to arrive at her apartment complex. He knocked on her apartment door. Nothing. He tried again. Pressing his ear to the door, he tried to listen to see if she was inside, ignoring him.

Edward went downstairs and found the apartment manager. He explained that he was worried about Emily Robinson and could he let him in to check on her? The manager, a stern-looking woman in her sixties who reminded Edward of an old-fashioned schoolteacher, took some convincing before she agreed.

"Don't touch anything, you hear?" she said when she unlocked the door and led him inside. "This is all private property, I don't care if you're her boss or not."

"I just want to see if she's here," he said, but as soon as he entered the room, he knew she had fled. There were no personal mementos anywhere. Just old tired furniture that looked ready for the junkyard.

"Did this place come furnished?" he asked, as he headed for her bedroom, half expecting to find her dead beside a bottle of pills.

"Yeah," the woman said, following on his heels. "It looks like she skedaddled."

He rounded the corner and saw the empty bed, stripped of sheets. The bathroom was equally barren. A quick trip to the kitchen showed some food still in the refrigerator and a few lone cans in the cabinets.

"She has two weeks left on her rent—I wonder if she's coming back?" the landlord said.

"I doubt it. But don't touch anything for now. Maybe she'll turn up." He didn't believe it himself.

He left and walked back to his car, his conscience doing a number on his brain. *You fool! You bastard! What kind of man are you, anyway!?*

He slipped in behind the wheel and sat, staring straight ahead. He pounded on the steering wheel.

Now what?

With nothing else to do, he drove back to the office. He found it hard to concentrate. Looking up his schedule, he noted he had several appointments outside the office that afternoon and didn't feel like making any of them. He forced himself to go through the motions. He didn't make a sale all day.

When he returned, Mrs. Dowd was waiting for him.

"Did you find her?'"

"Uh, no. She wasn't home," he said, leaving out the part about her apparently moving in the middle of the night. "Does she have any family around?"

"She didn't say. Why, do you think she went there?"

"I don't know. But I'd like to find her."

"Maybe she doesn't want to be found." Edward could hear the accusation in her voice.

"I don't know why not. We still owe her for a week's pay, don't we?"

"Yes. I get the feeling she doesn't care about that." She crossed her arms. "What the hell happened, anyway?"

"How should I know?" he bluffed and hoped she'd let it go.

"Clearly she was upset about something, to quit like that out of the blue."

"If I find her, I'll ask her," he said. "Um, can you give me her personnel file? Maybe I can find her."

Her eyes grew suspicious. "I don't think that would be a good idea, do you?"

"Well, uh, why not?"

"Because whatever is going on—and I'm sure I don't want to know about it—but I'll be damned if I'm going to help you find her if she wants to stay lost."

With that, she turned on her heels and left, leaving Edward staring after her, his face red.

***

The days crept by. Edward tried Emily's cell phone every day until one day, a mechanical voice informed him her service had been disconnected. In desperation, he phoned a private eye he knew and asked if he could track Emily down with just her name and last address. The PI, a shady character named Carpenter, said he could try.

"But Robinson's a very common name," he told him. "I really could use her Social Security number to narrow the search."

Edward didn't know how to get that without running afoul of Mrs. Dowd. "Do the best you can with that and I'll see about getting more information about Emily." It was just talk. No matter what schemes he cooked up, he came up empty with the stern-faced Mrs. Dowd.

Carpenter reported back a week later and said he was tracking several women named "Emily Robinson" but didn't have anything nailed down. Edward felt very depressed. He had ruined everything by fumbling around on his own, trying to pretend he was an experienced Dom when he really was just winging it. He had scared her off and she probably wouldn't ever be found.

Monday morning, more than two weeks after Emily fled, a new young woman was seated at her desk. She had auburn hair and bright green eyes, which were focused on her computer at the moment. He stopped, startled. "Who are you?" he demanded.

"Oh, hi! You must be Mr. Caudry!" she said brightly, flashing him a big smile.

Edward wasn't in the mood for smiles—and certainly not for any new girl.

"I'm Diane! I'm your new administrative assistant! I'm so looking forward to this job!" She was so chipper, it set his teeth on edge. He wondered if she would be as chipper once he had her bent over his desk. Even that image failed to lift his dark mood because it wasn't this girl he wanted in that position, it was Emily.

"Fine," he said and went into his office. He didn't have the heart to test her to see if she might be submissive. He just wanted to be left alone.

Diane, he soon found out, seemed to do everything wrong. She brought him coffee in a Styrofoam cup. She misspelled four words on her first letter for him and he didn't have the energy to threaten to fire her. He simply told her to do it right.

Edward stayed out of the office as much as he could, hating to see this interloper taking the place of his lovely Emily. God, he thought, if she knew how much he missed her, she might want to come back!

But that nagging voice within him said, *Come back to what? More abuse?*

"Shit," he muttered.

He knew what he needed to do and it rankled him to even think about it. It would be an admission of defeat and an opportunity for his hated rival to gloat. But he didn't know where else to turn for advice in this delicate matter.

He turned his car around and headed home. It was only two-thirty, but he figured he deserved a small break. He parked in the driveway and went inside. He strode to his desk and began fumbling among the papers. He knew he had kept Paul's number, not that he could easily explain why. Perhaps he thought he might one day call and check up on Adriana.

He found it and stared at the digits for a long time, trying to think of how to approach Paul. There was really no other way than directly. If the man wanted to gloat, so be it. He dialed.

"Hello? Mr. Antonelli's residence," came a soft voice that for one heart-wrenching moment Edward thought was Adriana.

"Uh, er, is Mr. Antonelli in?"

"May I ask who's calling?"

No, it was definitely not her, he decided with relief. "Yes, this is Edward Caudry."

"Will he know what this is about?"

"Probably not, but he knows me." He didn't elaborate.

"One moment, sir."

The phone was put on hold and he listened to the silence as he tried to visualize Paul's expression when he learned who was calling: A look of surprise, surely, and perhaps a sly smile—the beginning of a gloat?

"Hello, Edward? Is that you?"

"Yes, Paul. It's me."

"Look, if you're calling to check on Adriana—"

"No," he interrupted. "No, I'm not. It's another matter."

"Really?" Edward could hear the surprise in Paul's voice. "What can I do for you?"

He sighed. This was the hard part, asking him for advice. "Uh, Paul, I need some help." He went on to describe his desire to learn more about how to be a good Dom, although he couldn't quite bring himself to explain why.

"Is this some kind of round-about attempt to try to steal Adriana away from me?"

Edward grew exasperated. "This has nothing to do with her!" He took a deep breath. "Look, you claim to be an expert in this. I'm clearly not, otherwise, I'd still be with her. But I'm past that now.…. I have my eye on a wonderful submissive, but I fear I might, uh, do the wrong thing, scare her away. I was wondering if you might give me some advice."

"Well, that's very interesting," Paul said. Edward tried to read the emotion behind the voice. He seemed to be stalling for time while he thought it through. "I'm not sure I can teach you everything you need to know."

"I'm not asking for that. I just need some advice on how to gauge one's control against a woman's fear of losing herself. Or something like that."

"Hmm."

"I'm willing to pay you, if that's what it takes."

"No, no—I figure I owe you that at least. Just as long as this is an educational expedition and not anything else."

"I told you, I've moved on from Adriana. But I admit, it has bothered me that she could so easily fall for you. You obviously offered her a life I could not. I figure if I learn more about how to do this stuff right, maybe I'll have better luck with this new sub."

"What's her name?"

Was he testing him? "Emily."

"Hmm. Tell you what. Why don't we meet at the Riverdale Club on the west side? Say about five-thirty?"

"Fine. I'll see you then."

Edward hung up and felt better for the first time. He hoped it wasn't too late for Emily—if he could find her—but at least he'd have a better understanding of how the submissive mind worked.

He returned to work and found another client letter on his desk. The new secretary had done better—this one only had two mistakes. Still, it was time he let her know what he expected of her. He called her in and waved the letter in the air.

"This kind of work is not acceptable," he said in his best Dom voice. "I don't know why no one seems to learn English anymore..."

Diane, her green eyes wide, burst into tears. Edward was caught off guard. "What—what?"

"I'm sorry, Mr. Caudry! I'll do better, I promise! Please don't yell at me!" She turned and fled before he could say anything else. He stared after her as she ran down the corridor to the restroom.

He put in a call to Mrs. Dowd. "What in god's name are you trying to do to me?"

"What? What's wrong?"

"My new secretary—you didn't know she was a crier?"

"Well, no, that sort of thing doesn't usually show up during a job interview," she said testily. "She came highly recommended. What did you do to her?"

"She can't spell and when I tried to correct her, she burst into tears and ran away! How can I get my work done?"

"I'll have a talk with her, Mr. Caudry. Please give her some time. You know how hard you are on secretaries."

He hung up and sat down, mystified. This was going to be a disaster.

CHAPTER SIXTEEN

Edward knew why Paul had wanted to meet him at the club, rather than at his house. He didn't want him to see Adriana and what she'd become. Edward could only imagine, if the glimpse he had of her last year was any indication. By now she's probably some sort of mindless drone, covered with tattoos and piercings. And welts.

Paul hadn't changed much. He was tall and quiet with a regal air about him that hinted at the strong Dom underneath. No wonder the girls fell for him. They love a mysterious man, Edward mused.

Paul rose to shake his hand and offered to buy Edward a drink. Since it was the least Paul could do for all the trauma he'd caused him, Edward accepted. They made small talk while waiting for their drinks to arrive and Edward purposely avoided any talk about Adriana. That was all in the past— Emily was in his future, he hoped.

"So, tell me what you'd like to know," Paul said, sipping on his single-malt scotch, his eyes steady on Edward.

He wasn't sure how much to reveal. He loathed telling Paul how he'd screwed up a good thing, but he knew he'd have to express his concerns about going too far and how to gauge a woman's needs.

"This girl, Emily," he said, choosing his words carefully. "She works for me. I've already determined that she's submissive, but I worry about scaring her off. I mean, I know how to be a Dom and all, sort of, but I don't always know how to read a woman."

"Ah, that's critical," he said. "A Dom has to be like a concert pianist—too heavy on the keys and the audience cringes. Too light and they get bored."

Edward's mouth twitched, for he knew he had been too "light on the keys" where Adriana had been concerned. "Right—but how can you tell?"

"A lot of it is instinct. That's not saying it can't be taught, of course." He paused. "Why don't you tell me what's really going on, hmm? I mean, we can talk for days about how to become a better Dom, but you clearly have a specific problem on your mind. Why don't we just get to it?"

Edward took a deep breath. "Shit. Okay. This girl. I'm afraid I've already scared her off." He described how he left her in his office naked to be found by the janitors and how she vanished the same night.

Paul, to his credit, didn't deride him or make him feel any worse that he already did. "Okay, the first rule is, don't leave your sub alone unless she's in a protected environment. You weren't there to save her, which made her feel abandoned. She could've been raped or murdered."

"I know! I forgot about the janitors!"

"But except for that one mistake—and it was a big one!— you really must've been making some good progress. Tell me, how far along was she?"

Edward briefly described their little punishment sessions and how she seemed to be enjoying being his little sex slave. Paul seemed impressed.

"You do have a natural instinct. You just have to listen more and put yourself in her position. Subs really do have a lot more power than most Doms think. A Dom can only go as far as his sub is willing to go. Any further, you risk ruining the sexual anticipation. It crosses the line into fear—fear of discovery, as in your case, or, what's worse, fear of the Dom himself."

"I hope she hasn't gotten to that point yet."

"I don't know. To leave town does indicate some level of fear of you. She felt betrayed, especially when you said you'd be back with her clothes and then failed to show. She lost her trust."

"I'm hoping I can get it back."

"You have to find her first, right?"

"I'm looking for her."

"My advice? Don't rush things. Take it slow. She may want to run when she sees you—or she may be happy to see you. But you have to be sincere in your apology. You could ruin it by trying to Dom her in that situation. You could tell her you made a mistake and that it won't happen again. But you have to let her come to you—you can't force her to return. You can only encourage her."

Edward nodded. "You make it sound so easy."

"At this point, it's not. What could be going on is her internal struggle—all submissives have them, of course. They want the life but it scares them. They go back and forth and a good Dom will ease them into it until it feels right." He caught Edward's expression and hurried on. "Don't beat yourself up over this. We all make mistakes in this way. Me too, by the way. I've scared off a few girls, early on."

"Really?" Edward was pleasantly surprised to hear Paul's admission.

"Yes. My guess is Emily had been trying to decide if she should be allowing this treatment by you, even though it excited her tremendously. This gaffe of yours triggered her conscience and told her what she was doing was not only wrong, but dangerous. So she ran."

Edward nodded. "Yeah. Do you think she might come back, assuming I can find her?"

"Can't say. It depends on her internal dialogue. Seeing you will no doubt stir up emotions. Fear, certainly. And shame. But it also will probably trigger love and need. She wants the life, even though it frightens her. You have to remember not to force anything. That will make her decision easy—she'll reject you."

"All right. So when I find her, I just talk. I get that. But when does the talking stop and the Domming begin? I mean, how will I know when the time is right to get back on track?"

"Observation. That's the best way I can advise you. Just observe her. Take it slow. Introduce some games into the mix and see how she reacts. But above all, protect her. Don't leave her vulnerable."

Edward finished his drink and stood. "Thanks, Paul."

He stood and shook Edward's hand. "I must say, I was surprised to hear from you and not have it be all about Adriana."

"Now that you've brought it up, how is she?"

"She's good. She seems to be enjoying herself."

Edward didn't want to ask more. He said his goodbyes and left, his mind in turmoil. It had been good advice, but he had to find Emily before anything could be done to fix their relationship.

CHAPTER SEVENTEEN

Two months passed, months that only sent Edward deeper into despair. Diane quit and was replaced by Susie. Edward was no more encouraged by Susie, although she was at least competent, but definitely not submissive. He tested her early on and from her defiant expression, he could tell she considered herself a strong woman who would take no guff from her boss. Rather than have her replaced with another incompetent, Edward tolerated her while he continued his search for Emily.

He met Carpenter for lunch to discuss the P.I.'s failure to locate his missing secretary.

"You're not helping much," Carpenter groused. He was a big beefy man, an ex-cop, who peppered his conversation with police terms. "You give me nuthin' but a perp's name and a common one at that, and you expect miracles."

"She's not a perp," Edward reminded him.

He shrugged. "Yeah, whatever. What I really need is her Social. Then I can work some magic."

"I've tried to get it, but Mrs. Dowd guards those personnel files like Cerberus."

"Who?"

"The three-headed dog that guards the gates of hell."

"Oh, right." He gave Edward a piercing look. "You try going around her?"

"What?"

"You know, sneaking in and taking a peek? It's not as if you're going to sell Social Security numbers to the Russians or sumthin'."

Edward grimaced. "I can't do that—it's illegal."

"Well, duh. But we've tried to do it the right way—which, as an ex-cop, I fully supported, you know. But by now, we're gonna have to admit defeat or try to be more creative in our thinkin'."

"More creative, huh? Is that what you'd call it?"

"No one would have to know. It's not like we're breaking into Watergate or anything. We won't get caught."

Edward sat up. "Really?" He shook his head. "But she keeps her office—and her filing cabinet—locked. How can we get in?"

"Man, you're such a straight arrow." He laughed. "Now, you didn't hear this from me, me being an upstanding citizen and all, but there are ways of getting into a locked office without leaving a trace."

"You mean, like picking the lock?" He had no idea how to do that.

"Duh. Takes a few seconds. In, out, bing-bam-boom."

"You expect me to do that?"

Carpenter smiled. "Well, for a small additional fee, I might be willing to help you..."

They met at Edward's office at seven-thirty. The janitors had come and gone and they had the floor to themselves. It had been absurdly easy. Carpenter brought a ring of keys with him. He found the brand name key that matched the lock and slipped it into the hole. Holding a small rubber-coated hammer in one hand and the key with the other, he tapped the key and twisted it at the same time. It took two tries, then the door unlocked.

"How did you do that?"

"Bump key," he said.

That meant nothing to Edward and Carpenter didn't seem willing to explain further. They entered the office and went to the filing cabinet. It was locked, as expected.

"Never fear," Carpenter said. He went to Mrs. Dowd's desk and began opening drawers. She had left her lap drawer unlocked and he quickly found a silver key with an unmarked tag on it. He held it up. "Let's try this one, shall we?"

It unlocked the cabinet at once.

"Shit," Edward marveled. "Why didn't we do this two months ago?"

Carpenter shrugged. "You had scruples, remember?"

Edward stepped back as Carpenter rooted through the files. He soon found Emily's W-2 form and jotted down her personal information. He closed and relocked the cabinet and returned the key to the drawer. Carpenter showed Edward the data he had written down.

"Piece of cake," he said.

Carpenter called the next day. "Your girl turned up in Kansas City. Hey, that's a song, isn't it?" He began singing: "Going to Kansas City, Kansas City here I come..."

"Okay, okay. Where in Kansas City?"

Carpenter read off an address. "Apparently, she's got herself another job, too." He read off another address.

Edward's heart sank. "All right, thanks."

***

It was three-hundred-fifty miles from St. Louis to Kansas City. Edward called in sick on a Friday and hit the interstate.

He arrived mid-afternoon and drove directly to Emily's work address. He sat out front and thought about how to handle their first meeting in months. He couldn't very well just show up in front of all those people. He would have to get her alone somehow. He consulted his map and found the address of her apartment. He got lost a couple of times before he spotted the apartment complex that Carpenter had told him about. It wasn't much—another aging unimaginative structure just like the one she had lived in before. He parked in the lot on the same side of the building where Emily's new apartment was and waited.

At five-thirty, Edward recognized her car as she pulled in. She parked and walked with her head down toward her building. His heart leapt just to see her. *What had happened to her in these last two months? Who had she met? What did she think about me? Does she hate me?*

He couldn't believe it, but he was really here. Now comes the hard part, he thought.

He waited a few minutes to give her time to unwind and headed upstairs. He was very nervous, which wasn't Dom-like at all, but it was real. He'd been a jerk and an idiot, putting her in danger like that. He wondered if the janitors had been telling the truth when they said they only demanded blowjobs from his sub.

His sub, he thought. *I have no right to think of her as mine now. Be careful.*

He stood outside her apartment door and took a deep breath. He knocked and waited. The door opened a crack and Emily's lovely face peered out. When she saw him, her eyes grew wide and her mouth dropped open.

"Please let me in," he said gently. "I'd like to talk to you."

She shook her head and tears fell from her eyes but she didn't slam the door in his face. He didn't try to force his way in, he just waited. After a few seconds, she opened the door and stepped back.

He went in past her and stood in the living room. He found a handkerchief in his pocket and passed it over to Emily, who daubed at her face.

"How-how did you find me?"

"I hired a private detective," he said.

"F-f-for me? Why?"

"I came to apologize. What I did was very wrong. It was stupid. You were in real danger and I shouldn't have done it. I forgot about the janitors. I returned about a half-hour after you left, and realized my mistake. I've been looking for you ever since."

She nodded and sat down on the couch and put her head in her hands. Edward came to her but feared touching her might send the wrong message. So he squatted down next to her and said softly, "I'm sorry. I know you must've been terrified, especially when that janitor came in to empty the trash." He hoped to draw her out so he could understand what truly happened that day.

Emily nodded, her face buried in the handkerchief. "I-I was scared. And m-mad at you," she said between sobs. "You said you'd be right back with my clothes!"

"I know." He bit his lip. "Look, I was enjoying myself a little too much. And you paid the price. It was a stupid thing to do and I'm very sorry it happened."

She nodded. Finally, she looked up at him. "I was so scared," she repeated.

"Can you tell me what happened?"

She shook her head quickly, back and forth. Edward didn't press. She would tell him in time—or not at all. He could only hope she might someday forgive him.

"All right," he said, trying to change the subject. "So you up and moved to Kansas City. Why here?"

"I have family here."

Edward looked around, wondering: So why is she living in this crappy apartment? She seemed to read his mind.

"My mother's remarried and I didn't want to impose on them, so I got my own place."

He nodded. "I hear you have a new job. How's that working out?"

Emily shrugged. "It's okay. I'm a secretary for another manufacturer."

"Is your boss nice?"

She wiggled her hand in the air. "He's okay. It's kinda boring, actually."

"Maybe boring is good, after your previous job."

"I can't believe you followed me here."

"Like I said, I was worried about you. And it was my fault."

"So that's all you wanted? Just to come and apologize?"

Was she fishing? Whatever the reason, Edward was happy for the opening. "No. I was hoping you might come back."

"To your office?"

"Well, yeah. But I would understand if that place had a bad memory for you now."

She nodded at once but her eyes seemed hopeful. That encouraged him. "I didn't come just because you were a good secretary—I came because I think we're a good fit."

Emily's teary eyes searched his face. She didn't speak but her eyes grew wide.

It was time to be honest and hope for the best, he thought. "Emily, I had another girlfriend, before you. She was a submissive too. I lost her to, uh, another man. Ever since, I'd been looking for someone just like you. A wonderful woman who had those same needs, same desires. And I ruined it. I don't think I ever told you how much you meant to me."

More tears flowed from Emily's eyes and Edward hoped they were tears of joy.

"I'd like you to come back and work for me. And let's see where things go from there, okay?"

She blinked her eyes and he saw another expression, a hardness he hadn't seen before.

"I..." she began. "I appreciate you coming by. I'm flattered. But I need time to think. I'd like you to go now."

So much for being the Dom in the relationship, he thought. He stood, trying to muster as much dignity he could from this disastrous situation. "Very well, Emily. I'll go. But I'm not giving up on you yet. I plan to write you and call you and I hope that someday, you'll understand that I feel we were meant to be together."

He went to the door. She held up his handkerchief and he waved it away. "Keep it. I'll get it back someday." He left, trying to fight this own tears as he headed back to his car.

Well, that was a fine mess, he thought. *I ruined everything.*

CHAPTER EIGHTEEN

Edward threw himself into his job. He made more sales in the following month than he had in the previous two months and management was pleased. He accepted their congratulations, but his heart wasn't in it.

As much as he had tried to reach out to Emily, she had resisted him. Their phone conversations were strained and often she didn't pick up the phone at all. He had no doubt she was there, listening to his voice on the answering machine. It was as if she was stuck, torn between her needs and her fear.

Edward was about to give up, thinking she would never allow herself to be under his control again. Before he took that final step, he decided to pay one more visit to Paul. Maybe he could help him understand why she was being so reluctant. This time, it was easier for him to call the experienced Dom and they agreed to meet again at the club. Edward arrived first and was sipping his drink when Paul walked in.

"Edward! Nice to see you again." Paul stuck out his hand.

Edward shook it and nodded his greeting. "Thanks for agreeing to meet with me again. I'm at my wit's end."

"What seems to be the problem? We're still talking about Emily, right?"

"Right." He explained how he had gone to her and apologized and she had said she needed time.

"But that was more than a month ago and she won't budge. We talk on the phone now and then—when I can get through—and I think she still likes me, but she just doesn't seem to be able to move forward."

"Hmm." Paul steepled his fingers. "Interesting."

"What?"

"Let me ask you: Describe for me a typical phone conversation you've had with her in the last couple weeks."

"Uh, well, she'll say hello and I'll identify myself and we talk about her job or my company and then I'll ask her if she's feeling any better about me and if she'd consider coming back to work for me. Or even to live with me, if she'll have me."

"Ah, I think I see your problem."

"What do you mean?"

"Well, if Emily is as submissive as you say, she may be waiting for you to take charge again. She needs to feel protected, see—"

"And I violated that."

"Yes and you told her it was a mistake and that was fine. But now you're acting more like a lovesick boyfriend than a Dom, don't you see?"

Edward thought about that. The position of power had certainly changed. He realized he had given her the authority to make the decision about whether she would forgive him or come back to St. Louis. Slowly he began to nod his head.

"I think I see. But how do I know when she's ready? I mean, I made a mistake and I want to ease back into it. If I go back there and frighten her, I'll never get her back."

"Yes, it's tricky. You have to be able to read the signs. Watch her expression, watch her body language. That will tell you what she wants."

"I fear she might run away screaming or something."

"No, she's already done that. Moving three hundred miles away was her statement." He paused. "Do you think she's happy in her new place, her new job?"

"I don't know. She doesn't say much about it. I get the feeling it's just a job to her."

"Good. So she's working it out in her mind. She's safe but unfulfilled. What you have to do is show her that you offer that excitement she needs—without the danger. For now, anyway."

"What do you mean, 'for now'?"

"You've heard of a 'love-hate' relationship, right? Well, for subs, it's more like 'need-fear' relationship with their Dom. They fear you a little—that's what the punishments are all about. But it also excites them to no end. They need it. Once the accept your control in a loving way, you'll find you can push them further and further along until you reach their limit—or have them where you want them."

"And where is that?"

"That, my friend, is up to you. And her, of course. That's what's so fun about the lifestyle—exploring that edge where both parties are getting what they want, even if it's a little bit dangerous."

For the first time, Edward understood what must've been going on in Adriana's mind. He hadn't pushed her nearly enough. She had felt frustrated. So when Master Paul came along, she found a renewed excitement. Edward realized for the first time if he had acted more forcefully when she was wavering, she probably would've stayed with him.

But then he would not have found Emily.

"The subs really have a lot of power, don't they?"

"Yes and no. They have limits, and they'll tell you when you reach them. But they also need that subjugation—in a safe environment, of course. I'd say Emily is missing out on that. She's afraid, but that will fade with time. She'll want what she had, but not with the same intensity at first. Later on, you can explore her limits at your leisure."

"I'm still not entirely sure how to handle her now. I don't want to scare her away and I don't want to keep calling her if she's resisting me."

"Yes. What you need to do now, I think, is to start exerting your authority again. In small doses. Just give her a little push as you talk. It will reawaken her needs and if I'm right, you'll find her eager to talk to you as the days pass. You must show her that you're a real Dom, not some fumbling amateur."

"But I feel like an amateur!"

"You're new at it. I think your heart's in the right place. Go with your gut. Listen to her carefully. That's the best advice I can give you. Listen and believe in yourself."

On the way home, Edward thought about Paul's advice. It was true that he had almost abandoned his efforts at domination of her because he felt so guilty. Well, it was time to stop that. Don't be a jerk, but don't be a pushover. No sub wants a pushover.

That night, he called Emily. When she didn't answer, the machine picked up and Edward said, "Emily, it's me. I know you're there. Please pick up the phone. It's important."

His heart leapt when she obeyed him.

"Yes? I'm sorry, I was in the other room," she said and he knew it was probably a lie.

"How are you?"

"I'm fine. What's so important?"

"My secretary is thinking of leaving and I'm going to need a new one." He paused and let that information sink it. Susie hadn't said any such thing, but he could read the signs. She was becoming fed up with his quirky behavior and he doubted she'd last another month.

Emily didn't say anything. Edward could hear her breathing on the phone. "I would like you to come back and work for me."

"But I have a job," she said.

"Tell me about it."

"I told you. I'm just a secretary, like before."

"Tell me about your boss." She had never really gone into detail before.

"Uh, he's okay. Kinda quiet."

"Come on, Miss Robinson, you can do better than that." He was using his Dom voice but lightly so as to not to scare her away. "Describe him for me."

"He, uh, he's kinda fat. And distracted. He's got papers all over his desk all the time."

"Do you really prefer him to working for me?"

"Well, it's different."

"You know what you need. That job represents boredom and lack of fulfillment."

"It's not dangerous," she said pointedly.

Edward knew he was at a critical moment. He tried to think what Paul might say at this point. "Yes, we've gone over that. You already know it won't happen again. What you need to think about now is how much you miss the other parts of it."

Again she didn't speak but Edward thought her breathing came a little more quickly now.

"It excited you. It's all right to admit it."

"I...I don't..."

"Come on, be honest. It reached a part of you that you didn't know you had."

"It...it scared me."

"I know it did. But that's not all, is it?"

"Uh, no," she admitted.

"Sooner or later, you'll want to return to it. You'll seek it out. And your next 'boss' might not understand you as well as I do. He might scare you even more."

"I don't know. I have to think."

Edward felt it would be a mistake to let her off the hook so easily. "I want to see you this weekend."

"Wh-what?"

"This weekend? Do you have plans?"

"Well, uh, no."

"Good. I'll be over there early afternoon, Saturday."

"But Mr. Caudry—"

"Don't worry. I just want to talk to you. Okay? I'll see you then. Bye." He hung up before she could refuse him. She needed to be pushed a little. Paul was right. If he had kept to his "please forgive me" routine, he'd never win her back.

Now he had to figure out what to do when he went down there. That was going to take some thought.

CHAPTER NINETEEN

She opened the door and stared at him like she couldn't believe he was actually there. "Oh, hi," she said. She was dressed in jeans and a blue T-shirt. He could see the outline of her bra straps through the material.

"Let me in, please, Emily."

She moved aside and he went past her. Her apartment was very much the same as he remembered—dingy and small, but neatly kept.

"This is no way for you to live," he said at once, taking in the surroundings.

"It-it's all I need," she replied.

"No, it isn't, is it? I'm sure it's fine for right now, while you're hunkered down here like a wounded fawn, feeling sorry for yourself. But sooner or later, you'll wake up and realize you want to do better than this."

Her eyes and her posture told him he was right. Her eyes were big and round and she leaned forward a bit as if to hear him better. He mentally thanked Paul for his insights into reading a woman's body language.

"Fact is, I need better than what I've got too. Did you know I've gone through two secretaries in the three months you've been gone? I can hardly function around the office without you."

A slight smile tugged at the corners of her mouth. "Really? You really miss me?"

"Of course I do! Why do you think I've been calling and coming down here? We were really starting to work well together."

She looked down at the rug, embarrassed. He could imagine her mind swirling with details of their little punishment sessions, her bottom propped up for his ruler and her mouth around his hard cock. He tipped his head and saw a pink blush creep up her neck.

He stepped closer. "I know I've pushed you hard. But I had to in order to understand you better. Now I feel that I can really give you want you need without frightening you. Can you understand that?"

She nodded. He reached in and tipped her head up and saw a single tear roll down her cheek. "It's okay," he said softly. "It's going to be okay."

He took her into his arms and held her there while she snuffled against his chest. When he let go, he held her at arm's length and said: "Now tell me about your current job. Does it really satisfy you?"

She shook her head. "My boss hardly pays any attention to me," she whispered.

"Yeah. Safe isn't what you want. You need attention. And discipline. And love."

More tears fell and she reached behind her to find the arm of a chair so she could sit down. Her body trembled.

Edward stood over her, gently stroking her shoulder. "Tell you what. Go in and give your two-weeks notice on Monday. I'll start the paperwork to bring you back to the office."

"But I gave up my apartment there! I have nowhere to live!"

"Oh, don't worry about that. You can stay in a spare room at my house until you can get yourself settled." Edward did not think she would ever need another apartment, but he didn't want her to feel he was moving too quickly.

"Oh, I couldn't do that!"

"Sure you could. I insist. It's the least I can do. Now, about this place. Did you sign a lease?"

She shook her head. "No, this is just month-to-month. I was going to look for a better place soon."

That told Edward a lot. Subconsciously, she wanted him to come get her. She just had to be convinced. "Good. Now you don't have to. Besides, this place isn't you."

She tipped her head. "Yeah, it is kind of a dump. But it's just temporary."

"All right. Get dressed. I'm taking you out for a late lunch. Are you hungry?"

"Yes." She turned and found her coat she'd draped over a chair. As she was slipping it on, she caught Edward shaking his head.

"What?"

"That will never do. You know what I want you to wear."

She froze, her mouth ajar. "You mean...?"

"Of course."

Emily stood there, as if trying to decide if he meant business. But when he reached into his inside pocket of his suit coat and pulled out the ruler he'd hidden there, she gasped.

"I think you've forgotten a lot in just three months."

"Wh-what do you want me to wear?"

"You know already."

She turned and disappeared into the bedroom. He sat on the couch and laid the ruler on the arm beside him. He tried to picture her back there, holding up dresses and skirts, trying to decide what might please him. Emily returned a few minutes later wearing a dark skirt and an ivory blouse. The material was thick enough so he could just barely tell that she wasn't wearing a bra. He didn't push it, for he was quite pleased.

"How do I look?"

He stood and approached her and noted how she seemed to hold herself in place when she probably wanted to fade back. He reached down and ran his hands under her skirt and felt bare skin. He gave her a big smile and tucked the ruler away.

She looked relieved.

"Come, let's go eat."

Edward wasn't familiar with Kansas City, but with her help, he managed to find the type of restaurant he wanted: Dimly lit, with booths as well as tables. The restaurant wasn't crowded. He asked for a booth in the back and was brought to a far corner. The maitre d' smiled at him as if he knew why he wanted such a secluded spot.

Edward was winging it. He knew anything he did carried a risk and he told himself to go slow. But she was with him and obeying his directives, so he decided to push a little bit, just to see her reaction.

After they slid into the booth, facing each other, Edward noted how the tablecloth helped cover her legs. He leaned forward and said in a firm but soft voice. "Emily, I'd like you to sit with your bare bottom directly on the seat."

She looked up, startled.

He waited a beat, staring at her. He gave her a small smile to show he was still the nice friendly Dom she remembered. But he was in control and she needed to know it.

She leaned forward and moved her skirt out of the way and sat back down. He breathed a silent sigh of relief even as he widened his smile and nodded.

They made small talk while looking over the menus. When the waiter arrived, Edward made a point of ordering for both of them: A sandwich for him and a salad for her, dressing on the side. Emily said nothing but her eyes seemed to take it all in.

He purposely didn't push her much after that. They ate their lunch and he paid the bill. He brought her back to her apartment and told her to pack a few things.

"What?"

"Pack just enough for overnight." He pretended to be exasperated. "You can't very well expect me to stay in this flea-bag, can you?" Her mouth came open. "I didn't think so," he continued. "We'll stay in a nice hotel for the night."

Her expression was priceless, caught between shock and delight. Finally she nodded and hurried off into the bedroom. Edward smiled and silently thanked Paul once more.

She returned with a small valise and he made her carry it to the car. She was still wearing her skirt and he told her to move it out of the way when she sat down. Emily took a quick look around to make sure she wasn't being watched before she obeyed. He caught a glimpse of her smooth haunches and wondered if she was still smooth between her legs. He would have to check that out.

He drove downtown, where he knew there would be several nice hotels. He turned to Emily. "Did you get on birth control pills like I asked?"

She turned toward him, eyes wide. "Uh..."

"Well?"

"Yes, sir," she said in a small voice.

"Good," he said, quite pleased. It told him a lot about her anticipation of this event. Perhaps she had dreamed that her macho boss would come rescue her from squalor.

He found a nice-looking hotel and parked in front. "Bring your bag." He went around and retrieved his from the trunk and together they went inside. He handed his keys to a valet and checked them both in. It was expensive and Edward slipped a glance over at Emily as she took everything in. He could tell she was impressed.

Good, he thought. Let her see what it might be like to stay with him.

The bellhop took their bags and they rode up to the sixth floor. The room was luxurious—even Edward was impressed. The suite was large, with a king-sized bed and comfortable furniture. The bellhop swept the window curtains aside, showing them a nice view of the downtown skyline. As soon as Edward saw Emily's reaction, he knew she was feeling much more comfortable with him.

He tipped the bellhop and closed the door, leaving them alone once again.

"What do you think?"

"It's wonderful!" she replied, twirling around. "It's beautiful!"

"Glad you like it. Consider this your employee incentive."

She stopped and gazed at him. He thought for a moment he had pressed too far, but then she tipped her head and smiled. "It's very nice. I'll bet none of your other secretaries got this!"

He chuckled. "No, they didn't."

She went into the bathroom and he could hear her marveling about the tub. He followed her in and noted it was large enough for two easily. The spout poured from the center and it had a spray attachment—perfect for some couples' fun.

"I've never seen such a large tub!"

He reached down and turned on the taps. "In that case, we shall have a bath."

She looked up. "You mean, together?"

"Of course."

He turned away, ignoring her surprised expression. Did she really think they would not be naked and have sex tonight? He didn't want her to think too much about it. She had to learn just to go along with his wishes. She would find it would be quite rewarding.

He purposely did not allude to any punishments she had already chalked up—hesitating before changing her clothes or lifting her skirt to sit bare-assed—but he fully intended to bring them up eventually. Just take it slow, he told himself. Make her miss you and miss the lifestyle. Above all, relieve her of fear. She would have to learn to trust him all over again.

He twisted the taps and the water thundered out. He found some bubble bath salts among the hotel supplies and poured them in. Emily laughed when she saw the bubbles begin to fill the tub. They stood for a few minutes and watched the water rise. Edward bent down and adjusted the temperature until it was hot and steaming.

"Take off your clothes," he said nonchalantly. He began to strip.

Emily hesitated only for a moment before stripping down. He noted she did turn away from him, which seemed odd since he had seen her naked so many times before. He ignored her and slipped into the tub, sighing aloud at how relaxing it felt.

She stepped in and Edward could see she her pubic hair had started to grow in. He pointed. "That will have to go," he said before she could sit down.

She glanced down and quickly sat, hiding herself among the bubbles. He watched as she bit her lip, but she didn't say anything.

They washed and talked casually, as if they were having a drink in the living room, not naked in a tub together. Edward found it delightfully sexy and he could tell Emily did too.

He realized being a master meant more than just ordering a submissive around—it also meant being playful at times. He had been caught up in the game so much, he had lost sight of how much fun it can be—for both parties. Of course it had been fun for him, but he needed to think more about her needs—and fears.

Edward felt he had reached a better understanding of what it was to be a Dom. From that point on, he decided he would be more relaxed about his efforts to learn the lifestyle. He'd been pushing, trying to force her into his image of what a perfect sub should be. He vowed to listen to her needs as well in order to make sure she felt loved and cared for.

"Turn around, I'll wash your back," he said.

She smiled and obeyed. He took the washcloth and rubbed her back, enjoying the intimacy. She seemed to purr under his hands.

"Here, lean back—I'll wash your hair."

She almost gasped her surprise. But she leaned against his upraised knees and he used the spray nozzle to wet her hair. Taking the small bottle of shampoo the hotel provided, he poured in a handful and began working it in.

"Hmmm," Emily breathed.

Edward felt her body relax against him.

"See how much better this is?"

"You're being very nice," she admitted.

"I hated to lose you. Everything was going so well." He caught himself before he apologized again, remembering Paul's words. "I'm sure we can get back there again."

She didn't speak. He washed her hair and rinsed it and turned her around to wash her breasts, even though they were already clean. He liked the feel of her nipples in his hand and from her expression, he could tell she did too. Emily returned the favor, washing his back, although he insisted in washing his own hair.

"Come on, let's get out."

Edward helped her step from the tub and used a big towel to dry her off. She stood naked, her eyes half closed, enjoying being ministered to. As he dried himself off, he pointed to the downy hair on her pussy. "Shave that. You can use my razor."

She looked down. "Oh."

He watched, pleased, as she went at once to the sink and gathered the materials. She glanced around as if trying to decide the best spot. She sat on the toilet lid and spread her legs wide. Her self-consciousness from earlier seemed to have vanished. He didn't want to make her feel nervous, so he only stole glances now and then as she bent down and spread the foam over her mound and began to shave. He brushed his teeth and combed his hair, taking his time so he could keep an eye on her.

She finished and stood up. "There."

He turned and let his gaze fasten on her bare pussy. "Good. Very good."

She brushed her teeth and followed him into the bedroom. He pulled back the covers and sat on the bed, naked. Emily was nervous. She waited for him to give her direction. He reached to the end of the bed where his suit coat lay and retrieved the ruler. Her eyes went wide.

"Lay over my knees," he said.

"But-but…"

"You can't tell me you don't deserve punishment."

"Well, I—"

"Leaving me without a word? Running off back home? That's worth a few swats at least."

"But I was scared!"

He softened his voice. "I know you were. But you must realize you can talk to me anytime. You can express your fears and I will listen." He patted his knees.

She came to him then and lay over his thighs. His erection poked her in the stomach and she had to wiggle about to get comfortable. He raised the ruler and gave her a smack on her pale bottom. She jerked and he admired the red mark it left.

"That's one," he said.

He gave her nine more, not too hard. He barely left red marks. She needed it, he knew. He eased her off his legs and she fell to her knees, one hand rubbing her sore ass.

"Now be a good girl and give me a blowjob," he said.

She looked at him through loving eyes. Licking her lips, she bent forward and took his hard member into her mouth. Edward was in heaven. Her technique was excellent. He stopped her before he came—he wanted to make love to her today. They crawled into bed. She winced when her sore bottom came into contact with the sheets and Edward ignored it.

He began to kiss her neck as his fingers roamed over her hot flesh. She gave a little moan deep in her throat. Taking his time, he wanted her to really feel the love between them. Yes, he was her Dom, but he was also her lover and he cared about her feelings. He moved down and kissed her nipples, feeling them reach out in response. His kisses continued down her stomach and she gasped in surprise when he spread her legs and began to tongue her in her private place.

"Oh! Oh, Mr. Caudry!" Her hands fluttered about as if to pull him back up to her. He ignored her and quickly brought her to a satisfying climax.

The climbed up over her. Emily's eyes grew wide. "Oh my."

"You were a very bad girl, you know," he said, letting his cock barely slip between the cleft of her pussy.

She nodded.

"Running off like that." More of his cock slipped in. Her mouth came open.

"You needed that spanking."

She nodded now, her breath catching in her throat.

"Didn't you?"

"Y-yes, sir," she breathed, losing herself in his thrusts.

He pressed himself all the way in, feeling her warm pussy envelope him. He drew back and pressed forward again, watching her eyes, her mouth. Her face grew flushed as he increased his thrusts. She hung on to him as his cock pistoned inside her. Her breath rose in octaves until she was hanging on as she cried out her pleasure.

"OH! OH! OH!"

She climaxed and Edward felt his cock explode. Sparks danced in his vision and at that moment, he felt an amazing connection to this young woman. Emotionally, they were one for a split second and he hung onto that before it faded and he sank down to rest his head in the crook of her neck.

"Oh my," she whispered.

"That was wonderful," he agreed.

CHAPTER TWENTY

Sunday afternoon, Edward drove home, feeling pleased with how the weekend had gone. They had made love many times since that first time early Saturday afternoon. Their relationship had been more like lovers than Dom-sub and Edward did wonder about that. Did he want a girlfriend or a submissive? He wanted both, he decided. Emily wanted to be with a strong man as well, so they did fit well together.

Just to be sure she understood her position in their relationship, he spanked her again Sunday morning after she had complained when he made her wear a blouse that showed a bit too much of her nipples. They had been heading out to brunch and she had recoiled.

"But people will see me!"

He dragged her over to the couch, lifted her skirt, and gave her several hard swats with his hand. When he was finished, he said, "I like people to look at you. It pleases me."

She had given him no other argument. At the restaurant, she blushed pink whenever the waiter approached, his eyes widening in surprise, and Edward smiled at her and nodded as if to say, "Yes, this is what I want."

She had promised to give her notice Monday. Edward returned to St. Louis, mulling over how he might convince Susie to quit. It wouldn't be hard. He could just act more like a jerk.

It worked out perfectly. She quit at the end of the week. Mrs. Dowd was not pleased when Susie stomped over to her desk and announced she was leaving. She called him at once to complain.

"I despair at getting anyone to work for you," she said. "Can't you stop being such a hard case? You're making my job miserable!"

"Not to worry, Mrs. Dowd. Emily Robinson would like to come back."

Her voice faltered. "E-Emily?"

"Yes, she called the other day and said she was sorry she left—she had a family emergency of some sort. She wondered if she might return and I said it would be all right."

"Well, that's...that's good news, I guess."

"She should be able to start next week, I'm told. I'll let you know."

"Very well. It does solve the problem of this paycheck I've been keeping for her."

"Yes, it does." He hung up, feeling pleased with himself.

***

Sunday afternoon, two weeks later. Emily arrived from Kansas City, her car bulging with her belongings. She seemed nervous and shy and Edward remained reserved but friendly. She seemed wary about moving into his home. Edward tried to allay her fears. He knew she was still skittish.

"Our relationship is changing, I know. For now, you may sleep upstairs," he told her. "Come, I'll help you get settled." He dragged a heavy suitcase upstairs as she carried an armful of clothes still on their hangers. He showed her the comfortable double bed and the dresser and led her to the bathroom across the hall. She seemed in awe of his house and kept nodding at everything.

"Do you like it?"

"It's very nice," she said.

Edward knew his house was several steps up from her dingy apartment. Still, her expression seemed to indicate she thought she might be making a mistake.

"Don't worry, you can move out anytime. I just know it's not easy trying to reestablish oneself."

She nodded. "Yeah. Thanks, I appreciate it." It was clear she was wondering what their relationship might be like now that she was living with him.

Truth was, Edward didn't really know either. He knew what he wanted, but that would take time. For now, he was just happy to have her around.

"Come, let's get the rest of the things from your car and I'll make us some lunch."

It took just twenty more minutes to haul everything upstairs. She didn't have much. He left her to sort out her belongings while he made lunch. He couldn't stop smiling. She came down, still dressed in the jeans and a T-shirt she had arrived in. Edward studied her, thinking. Should he make a deal about her clothes? Or were things different now that she lived with him and yet wasn't his official submissive? It was a small matter—but an important one.

"Why don't you go upstairs and change while I finish putting lunch together," he said, although lunch was ready to be served.

Emily's eyes went to his and she froze for a moment in confusion. Slowly, she nodded as realization dawned. "Okay." She turned and went upstairs.

He puttered about, putting out soup and sandwiches, his ears cocked for her return. When she walked in, he turned and looked her over. She was beautiful, as always. Whenever he saw her, he was impressed, but when she wore a dress and skirt with no underwear, she looked even more stunning to him. Her dress was short and rust-colored and her blouse white. He could see her nipples through it. He gave her a big smile. She smiled back and he pulled back a chair.

"Sit, please."

She sat, tucking her skirt underneath her.

"Emily," he reminded her, still holding the back of her chair.

"Oh!" She lifted up her skirt and sat bare-assed on the chair. He scooted her up to the table. She waited after he sat down for him to serve himself first. He nodded his approval and took a sandwich half. He passed the plate to her and she took one.

"Thanks."

"You're welcome."

He picked up his spoon and began to eat. The soup was out of a can but it tasted quite good. Or maybe it was just the company. He glanced at her as she ate, feeling his cock harden.

"This is a low-sodium soup," he said to start the conversation. "It's very good for you."

She nodded. "It's good."

"And the sandwiches are portobello mushrooms and a low-fat cheese."

She took a bite. "It's good too."

Edward felt their conversation slipping toward inanity. He was so happy to have her back, he had forgotten how to be a Dom. He thought back to their time at the hotel and remembered how she had responded to him when he demanded more of her.

After lunch, he cleared up the dishes. She jumped in to help. When the kitchen was clean, he turned to her.

"Come, let's go sit on the couch. I have some things to say."

She looked at him questioningly, but obeyed without a word.

They sat, side by side. He took her hand. It felt hot to his touch.

"Emily, I want us to get back to where we were at work. Remember?"

She blushed and nodded.

"But here, while you're living with me, it's going to be different—at least at first. I think it's important for you to have a place where you feel safe. And I know you feel a bit strange, living here. You'll be seeing me 24/7. It might be a bit overwhelming. So please consider yourself my guest. I won't demand too much of you. Anytime you feel uncomfortable, you may use a safe word. Let's say, 'Kansas City.' Okay?"

She nodded, gratitude in her eyes. "T-thank you, uh, sir."

"'Sir' is fine at work. You can call me Edward at home."

"T-thanks, Edward." The word sounded strange on her lips. She gave him a tentative smile.

"You're free to come and go and do things you'd normally do. Please consider my house yours."

"Just until I can afford my own place," she put in.

He nodded. "Sure."

Edward treated her like a roommate, not a lover. He wondered if it was the right play and wished he had Paul's advice on the matter. But it just felt right and he went with it. Give her time to adjust. There would be plenty of time for fun and games later.

That evening, after dinner, she went upstairs to finish unpacking and get ready for bed. She hesitated on the landing and Edward thought for a moment, she wanted to be invited into his bed. He simply smiled and wished her a good night.

When he went to bed, his heart felt light, knowing she was upstairs. He could imagine her, naked under the sheets, thinking about him.

***

Monday morning, Emily came down for breakfast, wearing a yellow dress. He could tell at once she was naked underneath. He smiled. Pouring her a cup of coffee, he noted that she lifted her dress so she could sit on her bare bottom.

Edward told her he had a late meeting with a client, so she should drive herself to work. He gave Emily a spare key. Her eyes widened at the gesture.

"Th-thanks," she said, dropping her eyes to the floor.

He lifted her chin. "You're welcome." He kissed her on the cheek.

She left first while he puttered about, cleaning up the kitchen. He couldn't seem to wipe a silly grin off his face. He drove in, listening to classical music and imagining how the day might go. At the office, he strode in, nodding at Emily. He tipped his head and she came in. She seemed puzzled. Of course he knew she was already naked underneath.

"Welcome back," he said.

"Thank you, sir."

"I'd like my blowjob now." He sat down.

She didn't appear at all put off by his command. It was as if they had started over. She came around his desk and knelt down. As she reached for his zipper, he caught her hands. She looked up, startled. He shook his head and raised an eyebrow.

"Oh!" she said and stood. It took her just seconds to unbutton her dress and toss it across his desk. He grinned and nodded. She knelt down and unzipped him. His cock sprang out. She took it into her mouth and he leaned forward and stroked her breasts. She made small noises in her throat.

Edward had been waiting a long time for this and he came quickly. She swallowed and sat back on her haunches, waiting. He smiled and said, "I'll take my coffee now."

She got dressed quickly and left. Edward turned to his list of daily appointments, a big grin on his face.

Later that afternoon, he headed out, telling Emily he would be home by six. She seemed stunned for a moment, then blurted out, "Would you, um, like some dinner when you get home?"

Edward stopped and turned toward her, a smile on his face. "Why, that would be nice. Thank you. But you don't have to cook, you know."

She nodded and gave him a sly smile back.

The client meeting went well, but it took longer than he expected. He didn't arrive home until six-thirty. He felt drained and tired but his attitude improved as soon as he stepped inside the door. The house smelled wonderful—she seemed to be cooking up some kind of stew.

Edward couldn't resist. "Honey, I'm home," he said, putting his coat in the closet and coming into the kitchen.

Emily was at the stove, wearing jeans and a tee-shirt, an apron tied around her. She turned and smiled. "Oh, hi. I thought I'd make beef stew. Is that all right?"

He came forward and kissed her on the cheek. "That's perfect. It's a good stew night."

She blushed. He knew she wasn't sure of their relationship. She probably didn't consider herself a girlfriend and yet, she was living with him and making love to him. By most definitions, she *was* his girlfriend. He suspected she knew that this was just a lull in their relationship—he would begin demanding more of her. Looking into her eyes, Edward could tell she wasn't sure what she thought of all that. She seemed nervous and a bit too eager to please. Good, he thought. That's what he wanted.

He made no comment about her outfit, although he would've preferred she had kept her work clothes on or put on a more casual skirt. He liked the idea of Emily naked when he arrived home. That would come later, he knew. When she served the stew and took off her apron, he smiled when he noticed she was not wearing a bra. She blushed when it became obvious he noticed—her nipples poked at her shirt.

They sat and ate. The stew was quite tasty.

"It's great, Emily. Where did you learn to cook?"

"Oh, my mom. She made sure I knew the basics. I just learned to follow recipes."

"Hats off to your mom, then."

They ate in silence for a few minutes. When Edward glanced up, Emily seemed to fidget.

"Is something wrong?"

"Un, no...It's just, all this," she said, waving her hand around. "I really appreciate you letting me stay."

"My pleasure. I really like having you here too."

"Thanks, but...I should try to find my own place."

Edward frowned. "We talked about that. You need to save up some money first, right? You have to have first and last month's rent and all." He had no intention of asking her to move out, but he wanted her to feel comfortable staying with him.

"I know, but...This is a bit strange, you know. I mean, you're my *boss*."

He reached out and put his hand over hers. "You think that's all it is? A boss who is helping out his secretary?"

She blushed. "Well, uh..."

"You know I need you in my life. And I think you need me. So let's just let things go for a while, okay?"

She nodded. He guessed she was happy to hear he needed her.

After dinner, they sat on the couch and sipped more wine. Edward put on some light jazz and Emily seemed to fidget. He wondered why until it suddenly hit him—he had always played jazz music during her punishments. She was feeling it viscerally. He smiled to himself.

"Well, I think I'm going to go to bed and read for a while," she said.

He nodded. "Very well. I'll see you in the morning."

She went up to bed. Edward sat and thought about what should be done next.

CHAPTER TWENTY-ONE

A week went by. Sometimes, Edward would drive Emily to work with him and other times, let her drive herself. During that week, he always approved of her outfits before they left the house. She seemed to grow accustomed to not wearing underwear.

That first week, Edward asked only for blowjobs at work. He didn't ask for them at home, preferring that she enjoy a certain amount of freedom. Nor did he ask that she sleep with him. She was free to go upstairs and hide out in her room at any time. He never went up there.

By the second week, Emily had visibly relaxed. They had fallen into a comfortable routine. She was his little secretary slave at work and treated like a guest at home. She wore what she wanted to around the house—as long as she didn't wear underwear, he was fine with it.

Emily began to cook dinner nearly every night. Edward considered himself a good cook, but Emily told him it made her feel she was contributing something to the household, since he wouldn't accept rent.

"You know, I get paid tomorrow," she said Thursday night as they sat in the living room sipping wine in front of the fireplace. "I might have enough to find my own place."

"Do you want to find your own place so soon?"

"Well, uh…" She bit her lip. "I don't want to impose."

"You think you're imposing?" He took her hand. "You are very important to me."

She smiled. "Thanks." She bit her lip.

He wanted to ask how she felt about him, but clearly she wasn't ready to share. He realized she was waiting for him to take the lead, act like the Dom he was and she needed. It was time to push her and see how she reacted. He got up and tossed another log on the fire, making the room warmer.

"Take off your clothes."

"W-what?"

"You heard me."

She got up, her hand shaking as she put down her glass. Kicking off her shoes, her fingers went to her pants and unbuttoned them. She had to work to slide them over her hips. Her eyes went to his and he simply stood there, his back to the fire. When she pulled the shirt off over her head, she was completely naked.

"I like you naked," he said.

She nodded and stared at the ground.

"Don't be shy. I like your body. Stand up straight."

She obeyed and her eyes danced across his face and then seemed to concentrate on the wall behind him. He let her stand there, twitching, as he took her in. Her body was soft and supple and sweet.

"I'd like you to sleep in my bed tonight," he said.

Emily's eyes jerked to his and she stared.

"Okay?"

She nodded and gave him a quick smile. "Okay."

They sat and chatted for a while longer, he fully dressed, Emily naked. She seemed a bit nervous and Edward guessed she was still unsure of her place. He would have to give her firm guidance, he decided. No more being the casual Dom!

He told her to go get her toothbrush and she rushed upstairs to comply. When she came down, still naked, he reached out and touched her arm and she stopped next to his chair. Her eyes questioned him and he smiled and pulled her close.

"You look lovely without clothes on," he said.

She blushed and he playfully slapped her on the rump. "Now go get ready for bed. I'll be in shortly."

He wanted to hurry in himself, but he forced himself to wait a half-hour, to give her time to anticipate their love-making. At last, Edward rose and went into the bedroom, his cock hard in his pants. When he opened the bedroom door, he saw Emily was in his bed, her large eyes peering at him over the covers. He smiled and went into the bathroom to get ready.

When he returned, he stopped at the end of the bed and slowly removed all his clothes. She watched his every move. Edward pulled back the covers and slipped inside, feeling the heat from her naked body. He snuggled close and whispered, "Warm me up."

She wrapped her body around his and he could feel his hard cock press against her hip. He adjusted his body until it was pressing against her stomach. When he looked into her eyes, he saw lust—and a question there. Did he love her? He nodded and kissed her soft lips. She buried her face into his neck.

He took his time making love to her. He kissed her all over, from her neck down to that special place of hers until Emily was crying out for release. He body was hot and she jerked her hips at him in impatience. He made her wait. He purposely only teased her clit with his tongue, preferring to give Emily her first orgasm that night with his hard cock. When he moved up to her face and gave her a kiss, she was hungry and clung to him, her body held tight against his. But he controlled their love-making.

When at last he slipped his cock inside her, she gasped and came at once, her head tossed back against the pillows and her body trembling with the power of it. He slowed his movements until she came down from her high and began stroking once again.

"Oh god," she whispered as she rose toward another climax.

He prolonged his own pleasure to give her a series of orgasms, one after another. Making love to her was so easy— they fit together perfectly. It was as if he was tuned to her frequency. When at last he began to speed up, Emily clung to him, making noises in her throat as his cock swelled within her. He gasped and came hard inside her and she tensed and climaxed as well. They held each other tightly. Edward soon felt himself drifting off to sleep and he fought it long enough to give her a kiss and said, "That was lovely."

She purred in his arms.

In the morning, Edward couldn't resist having a quickie with his warm and sexy lover. Emily eagerly joined with him and they both had a satisfying climax before he looked at the clock and announced, "I guess we'd better not be late, hmm?"

"No, I wouldn't want to get fired," she said.

They got up and went into the bathroom together, still naked. Emily glanced at the toilet and then at Edward. He laughed.

"What? You're shy all of a sudden? Want me to go first?"

She shrugged her shoulders and he stood and peed noisily while she turned on the shower. When he was done, he stepped into the warm water and let her take care of her business. She joined him a moment later, grinning and hugging him.

She was his girlfriend at that moment and Edward had a sudden revelation. The submissiveness was more like a game, he realized. Adriana had never been the woman for him because she was a true submissive, one who required a strong, firm master to guide her. Edward was more like an actor who took on a role now and then. That didn't mean he wasn't a true Dom when the time came. It simply meant they didn't have to live the life 24/7. That would be exhausting. That thought alone took a lot of pressure off of him and he grinned broadly.

"What's that about?" she asked, soaping up his chest.

"Oh, nothing. I'm just very happy to be me right now." He hugged her and she squealed when his soap coated her breasts.

***

On the way to his office that morning, Edward was startled to see Mrs. Dowd and two secretaries emptying out the storage closet. Boxes of pens and reams of paper were stacked up on two carts as the women busied themselves.

"What's all this?"

Mrs. Dowd turned to him, pushing her glasses up against the bridge of her nose. "Oh! Mr. Caudry! We're making this into an office."

"An office?" It looked hardly big enough for a desk and a chair.

"Yes, we're bursting at the seams here—haven't you noticed?"

He nodded. He had been aware the company's income had increased in the last year, largely due to him. That was good news. But putting people in storage closets would only be a temporary situation. Bonham Industries would have to expand—and soon.

"Yes, I guess I have," he said. He moved on toward his office.

Emily was already there. They had come separately because he had another late meeting. He nodded at her but did not ask her in. He was lost in thought as he breezed by, barely mumbling a hello.

At his desk, he stared at his calendar on the computer. He had a lot of appointments outside the office—as he did every week. It gave him ideas. Wonderful ideas that seemed to dovetail neatly together. He picked up the phone and dialed an extension.

Mrs. McDougal answered, three floors above his. "Mr. Andrews' office." Her voice was distant and imperious.

"Hello, this is Caudry. Is Mr. Andrews available today?"

"Oh, hello, Mr. Caudry!" Her voice softened at once. She knew who the top performers were in the building. "May I tell him what this is about?"

"Un, no. Just that I'd like to meet with him."

"Oh! Well. Let me check." The phone was put on hold and Edward listened to some classical music for a few seconds.

"Hello, Mr. Caudry? Mr. Andrews said he could see you this morning at ten, if that's all right with you."

He checked his calendar. "Yes, that will work. I'll see him then."

He hung up and buzzed Emily.

She came in at once, her eyes expectant. She waited in front of his desk, her hands already hovering over the buttons on her blouse, waiting for his command.

"I'd like a cup of coffee please," he said.

"Oh! Of course, Ed-, I mean Mr. Caudry." She turned and hurried out.

When she returned a few minutes later, Edward simply thanked her and dismissed her. She went out, her face showing her confusion. She missed giving him his morning blowjob, he realized. That was good. However, he was far too satiated to need one.

He made some phone calls and dictated one letter before it was time to go upstairs. He glanced at his image in the mirror and straightened his tie. He stepped out and told Emily he would be back in a half-hour or so.

Edward rode up in the elevator feeling giddy and excited for the first time in years. He realized he was finally over his disappointment and anger at losing Adriana. Emily was the only woman he wanted now. They were a much better fit.

He stepped off the elevator and strode to Mrs. McDougal's desk. She was a prune-faced woman in her mid-fifties, but highly competent. Her stern demeanor softened at once when she saw him.

"Hi, Mr. Caudry! Mr. Andrews is expecting you. Go right in." She even managed to give him a smile, but her face clearly wasn't used to it and she looked like a bride trying to smile for the congregation after her groom failed to show up.

He went past her to the thick oak door, turned the brass handle and went in. Mr. Andrews was sitting at the far end of his huge office, behind a desk the size of a pool table. He was a heavy-set man of about sixty, wearing a tight-fitting suit and Hermes tie. He had a full head of gray hair that some whispered was a toupee—if it was, it was an expensive one. When he spotted Edward, he stood and spread out his arms.

"Edward! So nice to see you again. I want you to know that I've been following your numbers and we couldn't be prouder of you!"

Edward came forward and Andrews stepped around his desk to shake Edward's hand. He had a firm grip, one expected of a captain of industry. "I hope everything's going well for you. Is there anything you need?"

"Well, yes, there is, Mr. Andrews. That's why I'm here."

"Well, sit, sit!" He waved his hand at two chairs flanking his desk and he took one of them. Edward sat and straightened his suit coat. Their knees almost touched. "Now, tell me what's on your mind."

"I know Bonham has been expanding rapidly in the last few months—"

"Thanks you to, my boy!" He puffed out his chest.

"Yes. I know you're running out of space for new workers."

"It's a temporary problem, Edward. I can't go into details right now, but we're working on something. We're hoping it will come together sometime next year."

"That's good to hear, but I have something that might help you in the short term."

"Really?" He leaned forward. "What is it?"

"As you know, I spend a great deal of my time out of the office on calls," he began.

"Yes, yes—and we really appreciate it! I know you're on track to reach two hundred percent of your sales quota this year!"

"Thank you, sir," he said. "But I got to thinking: Why do I need that fancy office?"

Andrews' bushy eyebrows shot up. "You want to give up your office?"

"Yes—if I can work out of my home."

Andrews sat back. "Really? How would that work?"

"I would ask the company to remodel my den at the front of my house—it would only need a minor upgrade, really. I'd put in a computer connected to the company's server and bring my secretary in to work from there. I'd need another phone line too. Then I could handle my appointments and do all the same things I do now, only in much more comfortable surroundings."

His boss frowned. "That's, um, unusual. What about coordinating with customer service after the sale?"

"I do most of that by phone anyway. Or I meet the rep at the client's office. Trust me, I've thought about this," he said, not telling Andrews that he had thought about it for about an hour. Still, he knew it would work. He especially liked the idea of having Emily with him and away from the prying eyes of co-workers. "You could monitor my sales and if they dipped, you could recall me."

"It's unusual," he said, tenting his fat fingers.

"It would make me happy," Edward went on, closing the sale. "And it would free up space. It's really a win-win. And I know you'd like to reward the salesmen who have been doing well—I'd suggest you give my office to Determan."

Andrews nodded. Edward knew Frank Determan had been selling over his quota as well, although he was still stuck in the cubicle farm. Perhaps that closet was being cleaned out for him.

"You've made an interesting point, Edward. But I wouldn't want your sales efforts to fall off. I mean, I couldn't very well move you back if I gave your office away, now could I?"

"If I failed, which I have no intention of doing, you could always put me back in a cubicle. That would spur me to make my quota, now wouldn't it?" He laughed and Andrews joined in.

"Well, you make a strong case. I'm not much one for telecommuting—I'm old school, as you know—but I have to say, Edward, you've earned the right to try something bold like this." He stood and Edward knew the meeting was over.

Andrews shook his hand. "Let me mull this over and talk to legal and I'll get back to you."

Edward thanked him and left, feeling a little bit taller. He knew Andrews would approve it—he'd have to or risk alienating his top performer. It would free up an office and give the company a little breathing room before they had to move to larger headquarters, which was a very expensive proposition.

When he returned to his office, he felt invigorated and powerful. He jerked his head at Emily. She jumped up to follow him inside.

"Strip," he said and she did, a smile on her face. He sat in his chair and stared at her, a grin on his face. "I'd like my blowjob now," he said.

CHAPTER TWENTY-TWO

Two months had passed since Edward's meeting in Andrews' office. His den had been remodeled to meet his specifications and his computer and phone had been tied into the company's equipment. In many ways, it was like working at the office. With one major difference.

He turned and took in the sight of his secretary. Emily was naked, seated behind her small desk in the corner of his office. Her hands were tied in front of her with soft cotton rope. She bit her lower lip in concentration as she typed up a letter on the computer—Edward found the trait endearing. She still made mistakes—Edward had caught her in one just this morning—and he suspected she did it on purpose. He didn't overreact to her errors, but he made sure she knew it was unacceptable. Her bottom was well marked from his ruler and she wore nipple clamps to "help her concentrate," he had told her.

"I'm done, Mr. Caudry," she said, looking up and catching him eyeing her. She blushed.

"Good. Let me see it."

She printed out the letter and brought it over, placing it on his large desk, her bound hands making the effort more difficult to place it precisely. He left it there for a few seconds while he gazed at her beauty. Since moving into his office into his home, Emily seemed to glow. It was very freeing now that they were alone. There was no more talk now about finding her own place. She still had her room upstairs, although she rarely used it. Still, it was a retreat for her and occasionally, she would head up there when she needed a break from their little games.

He picked up the letter and read through it. Perfect. He nodded. "Excellent, my dear. You really have no excuse for making any mistakes, now that you know what I demand."

"Yes, sir," she said, eyes downcast. He caught a slight smile tugging at the corners of her mouth.

"Turn around."

She obeyed at once, showing him the red marks on her sexy bottom. He felt his cock stiffen in his pants and he bit his lip. "I hope you've learned your lesson, young lady."

"Yes, sir, I have. I'm going to try really hard not to make mistakes," she said, turning her head over her shoulder. He noticed the glint in her eye.

"Good to hear. You know I hate to keep having to punish you."

"Oh, I know, sir."

The phone rang and she rushed to answer it. She perched on the edge of her desk, holding the phone to her ear with her bound hands, wiggling her legs. Edward knew it was for his benefit and he couldn't help but stare at her.

"Yes, Mr. Andrews, he's right here. I'll tell him." She bent down and punched the hold button with one hand and held up the receiver, one eyebrow raised.

Edward's ears perked up. His boss was calling! He punched the button on his phone. "Yes, Mr. Andrews, what can I do for you?"

"I'm just checking in to see how things are going over there at Bonham-West," he said, chuckling at his own weak joke.

"Everything's fine. I think it's working out well for both of us, isn't it?" He winked at Emily, who was still perched naked on her desk, watching him.

"Yes, I have to say, I'm very pleasantly surprised. I'm holding the latest sales figures—your totals have not dropped off a bit! I had my doubts, but you've proven to be right, so far."

Edward knew that "so far" was a warning but he wasn't worried. "Good to hear. How's Determan enjoying my old office?"

"Oh, his totals have soared! He hit one-hundred-sixty percent of quota already! He's a very happy camper."

"That's good to hear. Just think of how your sales will do when every salesman has his own office—or works out of his home!"

"Don't give me ideas! It's hard for an old-school guy like me to admit when he's wrong. But I figure we can save a bloody fortune if we allow a few more to do what you're doing and hold off on the expansion of the headquarters a couple more years."

"That's good news. I hope it works out for everyone."

"We'll see, Edward, we'll see. Well, I'll let you go. Just wanted to call and say, keep up the good work!"

"Thanks." He hung up and felt a sudden urge hit him. Something about showing the boss he was right always made him horny. "Secretary," he said, "I'd like my blowjob now."

She pushed herself off her desk and came to him. "I thought you might. You always do after you talk to Andrews."

She knelt down in front of him and freed his cock. Using her bound hands to stimulate him, she took him inside and soon had him groaning. God, he loved this woman! He came and she swallowed every drop.

Emily tucked his limp cock back into his pants and zipped him up. She returned to her desk, wiggling her hips at him enticingly. He followed her at once and pressed her up against the desk, his hand stealing between her legs. He rubbed her wetness, drawing a gasp from her. As usual, he only teased her. He liked her horny during the work hours so she could anticipate their love-making later.

Just before she toppled over the edge into her climax, he pulled back and she shook her body in frustration. "You're killing me," she whispered, but her voice teased.

"I know. Consider it discipline."

He made her lick his fingers and returned to his desk. He picked up the phone and called another client. As he talked, he kept his eyes on Emily as she sat at her desk, typing quietly. When he hung up, he said, "How about a little bell, hanging between your legs?"

She looked up, startled. "What?"

"I was thinking, you could use a small clit ring, something gold and expensive. And I could hang a small bell from it. That way, I could hear you approach."

Emily's eyes glazed over. "Uh…"

"Good, then it's all settled." He returned to his computer.

Edward wasn't sure if it was his promise to give her a clit ring, but something seemed to happen to her that evening, after work. She was much more attentive to him, more aroused, if possible. She sat close to him on the couch as they sipped cocktails. He had untied her so she could sip her drink comfortably. Her fingers would touch his thigh and it seemed she kept turning so her breasts would accidently brush his upper arm. When he glanced between her legs, it was obvious she was wet with desire.

"I think you need a spanking," he said, putting down his drink.

"What? Why?"

"Because I want to."

He pulled her naked body over his knee and gave her ten swats with his bare hand. It seemed to inflame her more, which he had expected. "What's gotten into you?" he teased when he eased her from his lap.

"I don't know," she said.

"Okay, let me guess." He pretended to think deep thoughts for a moment, then said, "You are very excited about the idea of having jewelry. It will be like a mark of belonging. I think I'd like to have the clit ring engraved…" He studied her and her eyes took on that glazed look again. Her breathing became shallow.

"It would say, 'My slave,' or something like that. "No," he said, snapping his fingers. "It will say, 'Edward's Secretary.'"

Her mouth came open. He reached out and touched a hard nipple and she leaned into his hand. "You will always belong to me, Emily. We were meant for each other, I hope you know that."

She nodded.

"Good. I don't want you to feel forced into anything."

Emily shook her head. "No, I…" She seemed to have trouble finding the words. "You are an amazing man, Edward Caudry. Sometimes I worry that you might turn out like my former fiancé." By now, Emily had told him all about Adam. "But that worry diminishes with each day. You are a completely different man. And I'm falling deeply in love with you."

He nodded, tears in his eyes. "I have loved you since the end of that first week of work. You've taught me a lot, about being a man and a lover. But the boss part—that was all me."

She laughed. "My god, I had never had a boss like you before."

"Good thing or you'd be living with him!"

"Yeah, maybe. You took me by surprise, that's for sure. I wasn't sure which way I was going there for a while."

"And now?"

"Now, I feel like two halves of the same coin. You challenge me, you love me, you take care of me." Her eyes twinkling, she added, "What more could a girl want?"

Printed in Great Britain
by Amazon